# Murders in Progress

Eldon Cene

ISBN 692705090
ISBN-13: 9780692705094

# DEDICATION

To cellmate #3915. Where are you now my maimed friend?

Look for all these books on the Magic Bean label.

Magic Bean Books

Plays by Carl Nelson:
*Into the Wild Blue Yonder*
*Personal Growth Through Copier Sales*
*Ollie's Day Out*

Essays by Carl Nelson:
*The Audience is a Mob*
*The Pyramid of Rational Thought and How It Leads to Extinction*

Non-fiction by Carl Nelson
*The Poet's (Forty Pound) Weight Loss Plan*

Poetry by Carl Nelson:
*A Poet's Past Lives*
*Shoving My Way Into the Conversation*
*I'm Forgetting Things in My Dreams*

Fiction by Eldon Cene
*Murders In Progress*
*The Cognitive Web*
*The Mind Wars*

All are currently available through Amazon books.

amazon.com/author/nelsoncarl

# CONTENTS

# ACKNOWLEDGMENTS

I'm sure Eldon would be quick to agree that extreme thanks be paid to our publisher, Magic Bean Books, for taking on what has turned out to be quite an undertaking - to resurrect this manuscript from blemished and torn copy and scraps of notes and letters left by Eldon himself. As estate executor I'm also responsible and take full responsibility for the addendums and inclusions and bridges of prose which have eventually pulled the entire trilogy together. The fallout of its publication, both politically and artistically, is something that is to be seen.

- Carl Nelson

# Gravel Road with Two Pick Ups

A grisly murder had occurred just down the road from where Joe worked afternoons as cashier at the Mini Mart. And then, just yesterday, the severed head had been found in a field just a quarter of a mile from the path Joe walked home alone after work in the late afternoon. The rumor was that the head had been severed with a large hunting knife, at least that was what the coroner was rumored to have said. So of course all of the hunters in the area were put on watch.

And since the head was that of a (formerly) comely woman, it was presumed the perpetrator was a man. And when two different makes of tire treads but just one brand of beer can were found at the scene, (plus cigarette butts which had been used to burn out the eyes - and then planted, 'arranged' actually, on the burns), everybody was looking for smokers who drove pickups, liked to hunt, and who drank beer.

This narrowed it to just about everybody in the area who had testicles… and several who didn't.

Joe sighed and inhaled deeply, as he set off down the narrow gravel strip of road which was part of the route between the Mini Mart and his home.

# Mowing the Lawn

Ramey, local dentist, (when he wasn't a practicing psychic) had a sudden vision and ran inside, dripping sweat, to call the Sheriff's hotline.

All he had seen for sure was what looked like the edge of an old oil drum, maybe six cows, and a pasture that it seemed he had passed on the way home

# Suspicious Cows

Stan knew that he had killed all of those women. But how did the cows know?

It made him angry the way women could insinuate themselves into his most personal feelings. Nothing was sacred. They had to look, and observe, and turn it over... ruminate over every LITTLE thing, from some little light-hearted comment, to an upturned gaze, to even a breath that was a just a SHADE deeper than the rest... and it was like his mind was a picnic basket for them to rummage through! Stan knew what perversities and abominations such a ruminating and placid demeanor could revel in revealing, and he hadn't wanted any part of it. F#$king cows!

He flicked his cigarette butt at the most condemning of them and the dumb old milker didn't even budge. 'They deserve to be extinct!' He thought. He briefly considered killing them - and butchering them too. But Bob's wife wanted him to pick up some milk.

He supposed he'd better.

# Does the Name 'Nancy Loomis' Mean Anything?

"Does the name Nancy Loomis mean anything?"

"Sir, do you have some information you wish to share with the Kimmel County Sherriff's Bureau?"

Ruth liked the word 'Bureau' better than the word 'Office'. It sounded vaguely Federal which, she felt, gave it more 'Oomph'. Sheriff Leland didn't. But Sherriff Leland never answered the phones. So Ruth figured the two of them were whoever she said they were.

"I don't know." Ramey was on a disposable cell phone he had picked up in the city. He had a cardboard box of them. After watching all of the TV shows he figured one could come in handy. And he had been right. He couldn't have these calls traced back to a practicing dentist. That could cause all sorts of difficulties. "I'm not certain, I mean." Ramey was looking out his car window at a flower stand. He was working his way, left to right, through the various hanging baskets of assorted flowers, slowly pronouncing the name of each. This seemed to keep the flashes of horrible imagery, terrible things really, from overwhelming his thoughts. "Petunia," he said softly. "Chry-san-themum"…

"Sir, you'll have to speak more loudly," Ruth said, sounding more than ordinarily annoyed. After all, this was Federal Business.

"I don't know!" Ramey shouted. Then tried to calm himself, moving onto the next hanging basket of florals. "Begonia... I mean, I'm not sure."

"What information is it that you wish to share with the Kimmell County Sherriff's Bureau, sir?" Ruth said again, mustering all of her authority. These 'informants' were so *flakey*. She had often told Sheriff Kimmel, 'sometimes I wish we could just haul them in and beat it out of them with a rock!', which had gotten a laugh. But she hadn't intended any levity. After all, she was the one in the trenches. *"Is there information that you wish to share* with the Kimmell County Sherriff's Bureau?" She growled more loudly, "Mr. Begonia?"

"I don't know. I mean, I'm not sure if I do or not. If the name Nancy Loomis means anything to you, that is, if it figures in a current, by that I mean an, *on-going* investigation, then, I figure, I do."

"I know what *current* means, Ramey," Ruth said, finally discarding all of her patience.

Ramey looked at the cell phone as if he had been cheated. He had asked the fellow in the city directly: 'Is this phone traceable?'

"How do you know, er, *think* you know my name?" Ramey asked, the disbelief creeping into his voice.

"You're my dentist!" Ruth barked. "Everybody around here knows your *name* Ramey."

Ramey flushed. "Well fine then!"

"What is it you want Ramey? … for the fourth time."

"I need to know if the name Nancy Loomis, figures in any *way* into your investigation," Ramey's voice trailed off softly, "of the recent murders…"

"I'm sorry sir, but …."

"Ruth, it's *me*, Ramey!"

"And I told you, I know who you are, Ramey. But we can't reveal any information of an ongoing investigation."

"Well then, for Pete's sake, Ruth. Just tell me if the name *Nan-cy Loo-mis* figures in any way in what is currently happening in the investigation or even anything there at the Sherriff's Office."

"Sheriff's Bureau. And that would reveal information. This phone is for incoming information, tips and leads only. Now if you would like to leave a tip or a lead, or any other information you may have or know of relating to the current *investigation*, I would be happy to write it down and relay it to Sherriff Leland. Do you have any of that information?"

"I don't know!"

"Well then, perhaps you could call us back when you do know, sir."

"That's not my job, that's *your* job," Ramey pointed out.

"Are you phoning to tell me my job Ramey?" Ruth's voice went from Passive Aggressive Bureaucratese to actively hostile in a quick second. Which was a relief, Ramey felt.

Ramey quickly said the names of three more flowers.

"Okay, *Ruth*. Let's do it this way. You're into me for $300. of past dental work and have two old fillings with deteriorating crowns coming up that could fracture any second, given the nature of this 'fractious' conversation. Now do you really want to give the only practicing dentist within 50 miles - as the crow flies - trouble?"

"Are you trying to threaten a Federal officer, sir?!"

"YES!" Ramey barked. You didn't stay in a dental practice long without learning to play trump.

Ruth ground her teeth, then stopped, remembering what Ramey had just said. Ramey could hear her polished nails clicking on the desk as she thought it through. The one with the big phony rock on mid-finger struck loudest and last.

"Okay Ramey," Ruth said. "I'll give Sherriff Leland the message."

The finger with the big rock on it struck once again. Then, dial tone… Ramey smiled. Sheriff Leland was a patient with a lot of gum problems. He'd get back.

# Cow Birds

'Sound suppressor'..., Bob swished this around in his brain, taking another swig of the warming beer. That's what the guys down at the gun shop had called them, but Bob didn't know. They were kinda nerdy and over-educated... one of 'em wearin' special glasses and glancing real close at things. Ever since he'd been a kid glued to the TV it had been a "silencer".

He supposed he had all afternoon to decide, 'Silencer or Sound Suppressor'. Or longer than that. He could take longer. Sure he could. He could take as long as he wanted. 'A guy with a Sound Suppressor is his own man,' Bob figured as he shot another cow bird off the peak of his barn.

"This sound suppressor sure works. Used to be with one shot, the birds 'ould spook, and he'd had to wait a coon's age for another'n," Bob said to his imaginary buddy in the empty lawn chair nearby. "An' then one more shot an that'n 'ld spook! It made for a long afternoon and a lotta beer. But with this here sound suppressor," he popped off another round after setting his beer carefully and sighting like a sniper and barely breathing, "they just fell of the peak of that roof like they was in a shootin' gallery and he wuz takin' all the stuffed teddy bears like they wuz just handin 'em out." Bob grinned, so pleased with himself an' full of beers, that he fully imagined his imaginary buddy grinning back. 'Damn! I like this thing,' Bob thought, 'even though it don't make no noise, to speak of.' Harriet stuck her head out of the house to say something, and Bob pointed the gun at her... just in fun. And she pulled her head back in.

And after about "number 15" cow bird bit the dust, Bob decided that Sound Suppressor was what he was going to call it, 'nerdy' or not. 'It would make it sound more technical, like them boys down at the gun shop, and it might even impress Stan,' thought Bob. 'Who could be mighty hard to impress, havin' shot a bunch of people an' all, an' gotten away with it. ..an' probably raped several.' Bob licked his lips… and felt that tingling in his groin.

'Man, we is livin' fast, ' thought Bob. 'Drinkin' beer, killin' cow birds, usin' a silen… Sound Suppressor!' Bob grinned wildly at his imaginary buddy again.

Ever since he had happened upon Stan his life had improved in so many ways, he could hardly sit still. "A person wouldn't normally think meeting a serial killer would have that effect on your life," Bob explained to his imaginary buddy. 'But that seemed to be the way it was. Nobody seemed to want Bob around for nothin' nohow. An' now all of a sudden he's got just about the most unusual friend ever.' Bob shot another cowbird, (Number 16), 'leavin' nothin' but a puff of feathers.' "Damn." Both Bob and his imaginary buddy just couldn't get the shit eatin' grins off of their faces. They just kept looking at each other, turning away, and then looking back at each other again.

"There's just the smallest whiff of a pop! an' then thet cowbird was nothin' but feathers," is how Bob would explain it to Stan later, with his palms open to emphasize, after they'd finished eatin' - with his silent wife keeping her own counsel - over the emptying dinner table dishes. 'Ya just couldn't get her excited over nothin'.'

'Well, not entirely silent,' Bob corrected himself, recollecting the event. 'There's this great little 'pop!'.

"You point that there gun there at me again, an' you're goin' encounter someone shootin' BACK, Sound Suppressor or no," Harriet had said with an angry twist of her head, glancing back as she bussed the dishes away. "An' I won't be aimin' to miss.'

"You gonna take that from her?" Stan said. Which gave Bob a little chill watching Stan. Bob could tell Stan hadn't liked it.

"Well. Yeah. I guess so," Bob said.

"You gotta understan' how marriages work." Bob defended himself to Stan later, trailing him up into the hired hand's loft. "It's a little give here, and a little give there that makes the whole thing work."

Stan snorted, but never looked up from this plexi-glass case of curios and specimens 'or somethin' or other' he seemed to prize so highly, 'from the look of it,' thought Bob.

"Plus, she's a good cook and a good worker," Bob added, while thumbing through some yellowed and stained nudie magazines other of the hired men had left. "Plus…" Bob stopped turning the pages. "The durn woman can shoot the nose off a squirrel!"

Stan glanced up, a quizzical look appearing on his face.

# The Road Ahead…

Nancy Loomis was tired… bone tired. Some evening she was going to crack up navigating these narrow little country roads and end up as a quadriplegic running her company with a soda straw on an iPad. She squeezed her eyelids shut, *hard*, then opened them again. For a bit, she was focused and kept the sleek new Mercedes on track. Part of the problem was, 'the damn thing is far too comfortable'. She pushed the window levers lowering them one by one as the fresh air roared in. 'I should probably try sitting on a tack,' she thought, staring ahead at a straight stretch of road. 'A box of tacks,' she amended, finding herself enthralled by yet another urge to sleep … picturing a dreamy, and even alluring now box of tacks. 'They aren't really all that sharp at all!', she murmured, as her mind made itself all comfy in the buttery yellow leather seat.

Suddenly, the both headlights failed with a "pop! pop!" Nancy blinked several times, gripping the wheel tighter. She slowed the car while steering a steady course towards where she remembered the road as being. "It's incredible how fast a person can become wide awake, when you're scared shitless!" She exclaimed to no one in particular. As the car slowed, she brought it slowly over to where there was the crunch of gravel. She put it in Park, crunched the Emergency Brake and sighed. She had her cell half out of her pocket when she heard voices. "Shit!" she growled, fully awake. 'Those were *shots*'.

While searching for the speed dial on her cell, she reached for the Glock under the dash, just back and to the right of the ignition key. She'd thought she and Benny had reached an understanding, but apparently that wasn't the case. As soon as she had met the man, she had sized him up as an idiot! And had thought to herself at the time, 'I should be running away, fast.'

Nancy ran what she called "The Muffin Business", but which actually was a fairly substantial, five million annual gross revenues food accessories supply business - which had suffered an acute cash flow shortage in the downturn of 2008, forcing her to seek out a quick loan from Benny Green. 'You go into business with a bunch of losers and you don't bring them up to your level. They bring you down to theirs,' she grumbled silently for the umpteenth time. "And it's just problems, problems, problems!" She reached into the glove box to fish for a bullet magazine. This was taking too long and too many hands and she put the phone in her pocket while slamming the magazine into the gun butt. She felt better with the secure 'click'. 'The f#$ker couldn't work a computer; couldn't even understand a spread sheet. And now with this whole thing - if this is what it was - it was running about on level with the Keystone Kops. They *had* to be complete morons out there. Who else would work for that idiot?'

"Alright, alright!" Nancy shouted into the darkness, opening her door with her hands free. Her eyes had not yet adjusted to the dark. But she had the Glock in her linen jacket pocket and figured in a close quarters scuffle she was ahead against a rifle - if it came to that. "You've made your point. You can fire a rifle out of the darkened woods at a hundred and twenty pound woman who's half asleep and wake her up! And wreck her car! Tell Benny that's coming off my bill, by the way. And he can go to the police if he doesn't like it." Nancy Loomis peered forward. "Or sue me!" Her eyes had started to adjust and she could see what appeared to be the shapes of two fairly mid-sized men. She let her eyes roam so that her more light sensitive peripheral retinal areas came into play. At least they smelled of it! They were closer than she'd imagined. She put her hands on her hips, the one near her right pocket, and waited. The first person to speak in any negotiation was the less powerful.

"What do we do now?" the thicker set one asked as if he were truly bewildered.

Nancy guffawed, involuntarily.

"Shut up," the thinner said. And he moved so quickly that what with the darkness he was a blurrrrrr... Something smacked her in the side of the head. Possibly a rifle butt. And the next thing Nancy knew, she was on the ground with her hands bound and getting really scared. Her hose were ruined. Her knees were scraped. One shoe had come off. She screamed, loud! Loud as she possibly could.

'On the whole she didn't like women who screamed. But, on the *whole*, she didn't like the spot she was in.' The Glock was in her front pocket *away* from where her hands were tied behind her back. She stomped with the spiked heel of her right foot searching for the thinner fellow's instep, hard! as he pulled her up. But all she accomplished was the breaking of a heel. "Tell Benny that this is about the *stupidest* thing he has done to date. It's just plain idiocy!" She shouted while trying to catch the thinner fellow in the balls with her legs, backwards. "I've been making my payments. It's a *good* account!"

"Who's Benny?" The thinner fellow murmured, as he marched her off deeper into the woods. So quietly that she'd had to stop kicking and squirming, and ask him to repeat himself, to hear him.

"You're not with Benny?" Nancy queried. All of a sudden she was confused. *Really* confused.

"I don't know any Benny," the thicker fellow queried the thinner.

"No shit Sherlock."

"Just trying to get to the heart of it, that's all Stan," says the thicker fellow.

"Why don't you just show her our IDs?" The thinner fellow growled.

"What?" The thicker fellow said, puzzled. "Why would we do that?"

No answer.

"I didn't bring mine." The thicker fellow said.

No answer.

"It didn't seem like a good idea," he said apologetically. "You know, just in *case* we were caught, or something?"

"You're not with *Benny Green*?" Nancy couldn't believe it. 'If it weren't Benny, then *what in the world?*

12

# Publisher's Note to This Revised Edition

Eldon and I had to have a Publisher to Author 'conversation', which has led to the revised edition of this book.

"Eldon," I said. "We have to remove a portion of Chapter 6."

Eldon didn't say anything.

"I can't get it reviewed with portions of Chapter 6 in the book. The critic will not 'associate' themselves with 'this type of material' as a reviewer.

"It's about a series of murders, for Chr**sakes!"

"I know but the critic thought "it would be an interesting murder mystery".

"So why isn't it interesting?"

"Because he won't read it." Then I added parenthetically, "Nobody will. They all get partway through Chapter 6 and stop. One of my friends threw it across the room!"

"That's ideal! Just what I was hoping for."

"She didn't pick it up again."

There was a long pause, as I could tell this got to Eldon. "But he's got to be bad! Murder is horrid, for goodness sakes."

"I agree. I agree," I consoled him. "But more importantly than getting across to them how awful murder is - for our purposes - is getting them to read the book."

"What if I would agree to give 15% of the proceeds to women's shelters?"

"Eldon. Are you hiding in a woman's shelter?"

He didn't respond.

"Look," I said. "I've thought about it, and what if we do this?" I could hear Eldon wheezing into the phone as he anticipated my words. "We can remove a large portion of Chapter 6 in its entirety. Put the problem back onto the reader's plate. It's however they have it imagined. And then we pick up the tale in Chapter 7. I've tried it; flows smooth as silk."

Eldon tried to speak, but he couldn't. He must have run out of breath to spare.

"You're not lowering the price, are you?" He wheezed out finally.

"Once they've finished the book," I continued, "if they still have the desire to read this suppressed portion of Chapter 6, I will direct them to *a website where the material is available - just as you have written it. Doesn't that seem reasonable, given the circumstances?"*

*I heard Eldon inhale. "Do I have a choice?"*

*"Not really," I said. "Usually, by the time the publisher has this sort of conversation, the decision has been made."*

*"Good Lord," Eldon said. "It's just like prison."*

# The Only Law Within 50 Miles

Leland was heading out the door when Ruth caught him. He had a list of known sex offenders he intended to question first, and then the farmers who lived round the area where the decapitated corpse was found. The body and physical evidence found at the scene had been sent off to the county lab, and he was still awaiting the results on that, which he wasn't too optimistic about. The county corner was an elected position. And theirs was also Mayor, Postman, Building and Roads Inspector, and was promoting his wife for State Representative to boot. In short, he was an over-promising quadruple dipper. So that if Leland got back an autopsy with a finding with more than cause of death as, "corpse is missing head", he would be greatly surprised. If anybody was going to stop the dead bodies from popping up around here, it was not going to be their coroner.

"Ramey, the Dentist, called again," Ruth said.

"You mean our "only one within fifty miles as the crow flies"?" Leland stopped in the doorway to stand for a moment with his eyelids shut.

"That would be the one. And he sounds pretty broken up, this time Leland. All blubbery and crying, I think, from what it sounded like over the phone. He's a mess, it sounds like."

"Yeah?"

"Yeah. You might want to have a talk with him."

"I would, but he's called at an awkward time," Leland nodded. "Tell him that I'm tied up at the moment with someone out there who is not extracting teeth… he's extracting whole heads. And as the "only the practicing dentist within fifty miles as the crow flies", he should appreciate the severity of that. So tell Ramey that the only *law within fifty miles as the crow flies* is out trying to nail this asshole - and will talk to Ramey when he gets back! Maybe!"

Leland let the door slam as he left.

"Gotcha," Ruth answered.

Leland had already questioned two former sex offenders by mid-morning, and he was on his way to the third when he passed the fancy Mercedes left parked on the highway side. It was a nice day and there were lots of flowers roadside, so Leland hadn't thought much of it until he'd trolled past, moving slowly and noticed that both front headlights were broken.

He had been mulling over the two interviews he'd just given. He'd asked all the appropriate questions and written down their alibis and answers, which they had signed off on. But what he'd really been looking for was evidence that they had a buddy or access to a pickup truck, and neither had. In fact, both appeared to be broke, jobless, all alone and depressed, not even having the energy to argue. It had been all Leland could do to get the second one to speak at all. And then, once the unshaven guy had started, he just gushed - even trying to extend the visit with some "right-out-of-the-oven brownies" and chasing him right down the steps and back into his patrol car with a hot pad and a pan full.

Physical evidence can sometimes come as a relief! Especially the kind with that soft leather interior you can smell. So, it was a more relaxed Leland that turned the car around and headed back to question the Mercedes.

'Well, usually,' he amended that thought. He saw the crows hovering above the trees off in the woods. Then he walked over to the Mercedes where he got a bad feeling. "Oh shit," he mouthed silently to himself and undid the snap to his holster.

The headlights were not just broken. They had been shot out. Drawing his pistol he followed an obvious trail through the undergrowth and trees for about thirty yards until he came upon the scene of what was obviously another crime. Dried blood was everywhere. Leland put away his pistol. All that was left were the pickings…

He taped off the scene, called his friend Merlin, the local Vet, and bushwhacked his way back to the car, finding it locked. He scanned the car's interior. Nothing seemed amiss. It look Leland another ten or fifteen minutes to pop the locks and have a look inside. Nothing still seemed amiss. He checked the trunk. Nothing to see there. The dash box and other storage slots were all shut. Neat as a pin. Leland soon found the registration and had a look at it: 'Nancy Loomis'. The name gave Leland a chill, then a raging anger which tore right up through him.

"Ruth!" Leland growled on the phone. "When was it that Ramey left me that first message?"

"I don't know exactly. I can look it up. But it was a couple days ago."

"Do that. And call Ramey. Tell him I'd *love* to see him to have a chat, and soon! Ask him to drop by the office, if he would?"

"Gotcha Chief." Ruth always called Leland, Chief or *Boss,* when he was in that mood. And today, as much as she was able, she even tried to enunciate the capital letters.

# Merlin the Veterinarian

"What's up, Leland?" Merlin said. He had parked his Range Rover immediately behind the parked Mercedes. Leland handed Merlin some latex gloves and shoe booties. And while Merlin put them on Leland explained.

"Woman here, by the name of Nancy Loomis it appears, parks her new Mercedes by the side of the road after its headlights have been shot out. Then she gets led off into the woods by two guys, it appears." He motioned. "Try not to step on any of the footprints or to tromp on any of the evidence, of course." He rolled his hand. "They have a bit of a walk, and then she's murdered about 30 yards in."

Merlin whistled.

"I want you to have a look at her. Tell me what you think?"

"Okay." Merlin nodded. "Where's Pete, our Kimmel County Coroner?"

"Sister City Convention business," Leland replied, with a shake of his head.

"Aaahhh." Merlin said. "Love the government. Work hard. Always short-handed."

"Shut yer yap and just think about who's paying you," Leland retorted.

"Yessir." Merlin smirked.

Merlin kept his promise. He just whistled lowly when he saw the mess that was left.

The first thing Merlin did, after standing and studying the scene silently, was to set the rectal thermometer. Then he began to examine the wounds. "He broke her hand for some reason. Maybe she had a gun? Maybe some of this blood is theirs?"

Leland nodded. He'd checked the Mercedes while waiting for the Vet, and sure enough, there was an empty holding clip right behind the ignition. He silently thanked his good fortune that Pete was on that Sister Cities tour this week. Merlin was the much better deal.

"Sideswiped her." Merlin pointed to the grotesquely bent knee. "Probably in order to incapacitate her. Hands tied with a plastic tie." He probed around with his pencil. "Coat pocket ripped, burnt pencil-sized holes." He laughed. "Maybe that's where she carried her gun?" Leland nodded. Then Merlin began to examine the wounds. Finally, he stood.

"I had a schizophrenic who did his dog something like this, years ago," Merlin rubbed his face hard, as if to rub away the vision. "He thought the dog must have had some kind of a transmitter or walkie talkie hidden somewhere on it - because he said he could "hear the dog talking to him". So he went looking. Like this guy, he pushed his hands into the skull cavity and let the brains squeeze through his fingers as if they were clay, feeling for it." Merlin pantomimed it. "Apparently the dog had been bringing up some sore points and just wouldn't let it drop." Merlin glanced at Leland. "Could piss anyone off."

"Yeah." Leland scowled.

"The guy washed his hands, started taking his meds again, bought another dog and everything was fine." Merlin removed the rectal thermometer.

"So you're saying I should just hang this guy up by his balls and beat him with a stick until he promises to start taking his meds again," Leland growled.

"No. You need to shoot him. There's obviously two of them. Which means the guy's not off his meds. Or there is something else going on. Something much more long-standing, I'd say. Because he's able to recruit help. And I'm guessing he pays them with a little 'whoopee!'" Merlin nodded at the spread knees and the shredded clothing. "You really need to have the body examined though, and do the whole rape work up."

Leland nodded.

"Is that it?"

"You think I have another couple murders around here for you to look into?"

Merlin's eyebrows rose. He took a look at thermometer, then wiped it clean and put it away. "I figured she must have died about 12 hours ago." He sighed. "Can I go then? There's a dog who's breeching, and she's about 20 miles away."

"Sure. Get lost," Leland said.

"Will do." Merlin waved and walked off through the undergrowth.

Leland stayed to gaze around the scene and think some more. Then he trudged back out to the roadway to welcome the 'kids'.

The kids all poured out of the school van with wide eyes. Burt followed.

"Okay. Listen up!" Leland shouted. He didn't introduce himself because they all knew who he was, and he was wearing a badge besides. "You're not going to get to see the body. So I want you to just get that out of your thoughts right now." Leland had covered the corpse and head with a black body bag before leaving. The girls looked relieved. The one boy looked disappointed.

"There are a number of things which need doing and fairly quickly. The evidence at a crime scene can deteriorate or disappear quickly. So we all need to be quick, but thorough. We get no second chances," Leland declared. "I need someone to go over the Mercedes. Who wants to do that?"

The boy immediately raised his hand.

"Good. Now I need the two others to examine everywhere it appears there has been recent human activity for physical evidence - which I want you to pick away and put in these sealable baggies. This includes blood droppings, cigarette butts, lost items, hairs, fabric, etc. So you need to really look close. That means get your head down around the ground! And then you will record on this 'grid' we're creating where each of these evidences were located and write it on the side of the sealed bag. "

"I've already taken photographic shots of the area and crime scene. But if you see something you find remarkable, well then for goodness sakes, use some more film."

Ruth was there too and was handing out supplies. "We practiced lifting fingerprints on the way here," she told Leland. "And we went over how to walk around a crime scene; what to look for, etcetera."

"Thanks Ruth," Leland said.

The kids were putting on their gloves and booties, very quietly.

Leland took this time to grab Burt and walk him to where the two of them could maneuver Karen Loomis into the body bag, then pick her up and deposit her into the back of Sheriff Leland's sports utility vehicle. The kids all swiveled silently, following Leland and Burt's movements as the corpse passed by. Leland handed Ruth the keys. "Keep it under 50, Ruth. Tell Vern to put her in the freezer with the other corpse." Vern Smithers ran a mobile slaughterhouse with a wild game dressing and wrapping sideline out of his meat store where, now and then, the Sheriff's Office rented a freezer. "Don't use the siren."

Ruth gave him a look.

"Please," Leland added.

"Never any fricking fun," Ruth grumbled, leaving.

"I'll get a ride back with you and the kids if that's okay," Leland said.

Burt nodded.

"Well, that's about it," Leland said, hours later. The kids had scoured the area. Leland and Burt had made casts of the best of the boot prints. And they followed the broken underbrush but could find no readable tire impressions at the road site. Ruth had packed some sandwiches and Kool Aid. They drank all the Kool Aid, but no one ate much.

They were all piling onto the bus when the last girl in asked Leland if she could "write something about this for the school paper?" Leland looked at Burt. Burt thought it should be permissible.

"Okay," Leland said.

"And I would like access to a few of the photos taken, and a brief interview with you on the way back - if you would be agreeable?" The girl insisted.

Leland wondered why he hadn't noticed her pin point gaze and the firm set of her lips before. Leland sighed. He looked down.

"What's your last name?" He asked.

"You don't even know my first," she replied.

'My God, it's another Ruth,' he thought. "Okay. What's both your names?"

"Nancy Gillis," the girl replied.

Leland grunted. He couldn't place her amongst anyone of Ruth's kin and vintage. It seemed he remembered some Gillises lived out around Coventry Creek.

"And I intend to make a name for myself," she added.

Leland muttered.

Nancy Gillis followed him to the back of the bus, then back to the middle of the bus, and finally to a seat just behind where Leland sat down next to the one boy. Not such a good ploy really, because then Nancy yelled her questions across the back of the seat, so that the whole bus was a party to it.

# Out of Gas

The bus dropped Leland off at his Sheriff's office. Leland called Ramey, as Ruth tossed him the keys.

"Ramey!" Leland said, catching the keys.

"'I've put on a pair of flannel pajamas' and poured myself a big glass of wine and started a roaring fire and I'm just sitting here," Ramey lisp. "It's been quite a couple days!" Ramey blubbered.

"You sound *gay*,'" Leland said, completely thrown.

"I'm not leaving the house today, Leland. I need this quiet time to recoup, and to re-center! I feel I've undergone a horrible psychic invasion." Leland could hear the wine gurgle as it was poured.

"Ramey. I need to see you, now."

"And I don't see what good I could do for you there, *now*," Ramey spit it out like a mad cat. "It's all over *now*! It's too late. I've been deflowered. I just hope that monster didn't give me some kind of disease."

"Ramey, you get your ass in here right now, or I'm coming out there."

"You know, where was the *Law* when I came to *you*?" Ramey hissed. "Huh? You couldn't be bothered. You had pressing business. .."

"How do you know Nancy Loomis, Ramey?" Leland growled.

"What does it matter? It's too late now. I'm *dead*!"

"What?"

"You heard me. The monster beat me. God my jaw hurts. Then cut my head open, and pulled my brains out, and cut my head off…" Ramey cried shrilly. Then Leland heard the gurgle of more wine.

"How do imagine all that? …. Ramey? Are you there?!"

"Yes. So I'm just sitting here, curled up here, *now*, on my pillow … (gurgle)…ing this wine!" Ramey sighed. "And not going anywhere! Because let me tell *you*, I feel as if I'd been raked over the coals. I feel humiliated, and abused, and horribly battered, and sore

24

all… (gurgle) …and frankly," Ramey growled, "pissed as all Hell! I think, Leland.

"And I'm the only male *nearby*," Ramey whispered.

"What?"

" I'm really *worried*. Perhaps you *could* come out here, Leland. Because I'm really worried. She's saying terrible things, and swearing…"

"You're *both* there, at the house, right?"

"*I'm* not going anywhere," Ramey whined.

Leland believed him.

"I'll get there as soon as I can, Ramey," Leland promised. He didn't know whether to whisper or shout. So he did both, repeating himself twice.

Leland left the office, after leaving instructions with Ruth to call Doc Chatham and have him patched to the patrol car. Then Leland hit the lights on the squad car and with sirens screaming headed out of town. Three miles out, he ran out of gas.

"That damned Ruth!" Leland beat on the wheel. The patrol car was stopped by the side of the road, lights flashing.

Leland got out. As he stood there, he noticed what looked to be two guys approaching slowly in a faded pickup streaked with manure. Leland unsnapped his holster, as the pickup rattled to a stop there in the road beside.

"You got a problem there, Shair-eef?" Bob Weeds spit a slurry of tobacco juice out the window and smiled.

As it had approached, Leland realized it was just Bob Weeds with his Great Dane, 'Vomit', who always rode sidekick.

"No problem," Leland replied.

"Cause a lot of us was wonderin' whether or not you had made any progress on thet headless murder a week or so back, and hadn't heard anything. Some of us was thinkin', maybe yer investigation had run out of gas." Bob nodded at the can of gas. He looked about to laugh but bit it off with a glance from Leland.

Leland stepped around the truck, invading Bob's territory, and smacked the hood as he passed, smiling broadly. Bob jumped. Vomit started barking, and clawing at the dash and window.

"Shut up! Vomit. Vomit! Quit it! Damn it, would you shut up!!" Bob finally smacked the dog, and the dog squealed.

"Well, we just about got the head and neck connected Bob." Leland drilled Bob Weeds with his eyes, staring in the window.

"That's good." Bob nodded. "That's a start I guess."

"Yes it is, Bob."

"Uh, so good. Good," Bob said gruffly.

They did the stare down.

"Well, that's good. That's real good…" Bob mumbled as he turned his glance back to the roadway and put the truck into gear. "So we'll be seeing you now, Sheriff."

Leland waved - and Burt Weeds drove on. Then Leland started filling his tank with the spare 5 gallons he kept for stranded roadside motorists.

This was a bit of puzzling behavior for Bob Weeds to be exhibiting, Leland considered. He usually just slumped around with his head down doing whatever a hen-pecked dairy farmer did around here for a life and a livelihood. With few friends but a long family history in the valley, everyone knew who Bob Weeds was. There wasn't much more to it than that, usually. But it struck Leland now that he was acting downright cocky. 'And downright cocky was what usually proceeded downright arrested,' Leland considered, as he replaced the gas caps.

# The Feds

Likely enough Bob Weeds had been somewhere, where he had absorbed some 'growing community sentiment', Leland figured on his way back. He made it a mental floss to think a little bit more about Bob, and he put Ruth on the phones when he got back. Ruth was a master at 'salting the mine': just little tidbits of insider knowledge, just enough to let the local network of gossips share with the public at large that - at least in the Sheriff's office - events were bubbling, things were moving. Leland knew that in his job the campaigning never stopped. Plus, then Ruth could sift through the rumors which came back and maybe they'd come upon some useful information.

Five gallons of gas wasn't enough to get to Ramey's and back to town. So before Leland could get out to Ramey's, he first had to get back to town to fill the car and 5 gallon container. And while he was at it, he decided it might be best to stop back by the office to check on a few things.

"Ruth!" He shouted as he tossed back the entry door. "Fill that damned cruiser with gas after you use it." He tossed Ruth the keys.

Ruth skittered out.

Leland's first need was to change his firepower. Leland had figured the county issued pistol he carried was adequate for most of what he was required to do as part of his job as Kimmel County Sheriff. But this latest string of murders had larger troubles with a tag team of dual perpetrators written large all over it. And Leland imagined he'd need to blow a bigger hole through whomever it was doing it than a regulation pistol would allow.

After this second murder, a saying of Leland's Sergeant in the LA Police Department had come to mind. "You don't go hunting bear with a squirrel gun. Bigger game requires a bigger gun." His mentor had said that the morning before they went up against the Jamaicans. Leland had never seen so much blood. But it was Police

27

Department 10 / Jamaicans 0.  Lesson learned.

Leland sat at his desk cleaning and oiling and reassembling the 44 Colt Anaconda he'd fetched from back in the evidence locker.  He checked its action, and practiced moving it in and out of his holster while looking out onto the main street through the blinds.  Leland had been Sheriff ten years settling things like shot pet disputes, filched timber, and crop damage complaints when all of a sudden people were getting murdered.  It was changing how he looked out on Main Street.  And he didn't like it.

Leland turned back to oiling and working his gun.  He checked the sights.  He was figuring that anybody who was out murdering people might very well resist arrest, also.  And while he was thinking this and spinning the cylinder, something flashed in the window.  He looked up, 44 Magnum in hand, just soon enough to see a pair of pig-tails disappear.

He was thinking of giving the damned kid a chase, when an unmarked American sedan drove up and parked directly outside.  There was something about the speed and authority with which it parked.  Leland parted the venetian blind wider with a forefinger and saw a man and a woman in the front seats.  The man was talking.  They both wore dark suits.  Everything about this situation said, government.  And everything about that said, "Feds".  And everything about that raised flags.

Leland slid the gun and oils and clips and tools into his top drawer and wiped down the desktop.  He brought out a writing tablet and pen set with a little Smiley Face which said "Kimmel County Sheriff's Department, How Can We Improve Your Day?"  It was a little kitsch which Ruth had purchased.  It seemed appropriate.

As they poked their heads through the door, Leland noted that they were both carrying.  'It's funny how that was the first thing you noticed about somebody in this business,' Leland considered.

"Sherriff Leland, I'm guessing."  The man was 30-40ish, and looked fit.  He leaned over the desk and shook Leland's hand with the overbearing grip of an alpha male.

"That would be me," Leland admitted, while they ground knuckles for a while. "And who is this?" He turned to the younger woman, who was already working her way around his office looking at this, examining that.

"Agent Hailey," she said, and turned away, as if she had already revealed too much.

'Not a bad looking woman.' Leland's brows rose.

"And I'm Agent Curtiss, out of the FBI's Division office. Can we sit?"

"Please do." Sheriff Leland waved a hand.

"There are no chairs." Agent Hailey glanced around.

Leland chuckled. "That's how I keep people out of my office." Neither smiled.

"Plus, you know, it's the budget." Leland offered.

Not very believable really, but a shared gripe to be sure. They nodded.

Leland rose from behind his desk. "Usually when I really need to talk, I take it into the jail." He nodded towards the door they had come through, on the other side of which, Ruth grumbled, and returned to her desk. "It's more private."

Sheriff Leland led them into a cell, where he straddled a plastic chair while they sat on the steel bunk.

"Sounds like you've had a murder. A couple of murders here, actually." Agent Curtis began.

"Yes, we have."

"Any suspects?"

"Oh yeah. Nearly everybody."

"Everybody?"

"People don't live in the country because they enjoy each other a lot." Leland smiled. "In an out of the way area like this, grudges are made; they fester. This idea of burying the hatchet and making up happens maybe 5% of the time around here, except on evening TV sitcoms. Here, people fight, divorce, re-marry, or drink, and bear grudges well through three generations until someone runs amuck with a gun or a tractor. So when something like this happens *everybody's* got suspicions. I must have had about a thousand calls. Lots of tips. My guess is, that you're bringing me another. And you're FBI, so I'm thinking that you're going to tell me that this all has '*larger ramifications*'."

"That's right." Agent Curtis nodded. "We think that this latest homicide of Karen Loomis might be connected to the mobster Benny Green."

Agents Curtis and Hailey looked at Leland as if he might have something to add.

"You didn't say, ..."in some way"...".

"Huh?"

"You didn't say that it was connected in "some way" to the mobster Benny Green. So I'm guessing that you may have some hard information to offer," Leland said.

"Yes and no. Nancy Loomis was working for us."

"I heard she cooked muffins. You buy muffins?"

Agent Hailey huffed. "She was CEO of a *5 million dollar corporation* which produced Food Accessories."

"In a *big* way, I meant." Leland grinned at Agent Hailey. "So why would a woman who is so successful and doing so well be working as an informant for the FBI? That's pretty dirty, disagreeable work, isn't it? I mean, it tosses you in with all types. ...It's not the Rotary."

Agent Hailey shook her head.

"The recession," Agent Curtis smiled, leaned forward placing his elbows on his knees, and lowered his voice as if he were letting Leland in on a confidence.

The guy was a pretty good salesman Leland had to admit, except for that God awful grip.

"During the recession of 2008, credit streams dried up. It didn't matter who you were, and even very successful companies were scrambling to meet their cash flows. And that's where Benny Green comes in. He figures this is an excellent time to launder a lot of drug monies that otherwise he has to pay a huge commission to get pressed and cleaned. So he's out there helping out all he can. He comes across our Miss Loomis, and even though it is not love at first sight… they manage to work things out. Fine. But then two years in credit has loosened a bit, Nancy has bitten the bullet, cash flow has improved, and she's wanting out. But Benny doesn't want her out. He likes her where she is. And it's then that Nancy Loomis knows that she's stuck with this Benny Green whether she likes it or not. Which she doesn't. And being the plucky little 120 pound thing she was, she comes to us. And we reached an agreement."

"It was a very dicey negotiation," Agent Hailey cut in. "Because she was already up to her neck in legal shenanigans, and knew she was. But she also knew that they only way she would get herself and her company out of Benny Green's clutches was if we could somehow take him down."

"So we made a deal," Agent Curtis continued. "She helps us take Benny Green down, and we call it good. That was the deal."

"Only now she's dead." Agent Hailey said this with some real anger, looking as if Sherriff Leland had let it happen.

Leland looked at them as if to say, 'Then *you* must have gotten her killed.' It was a stalemate.

"It doesn't look like a mob killing," Leland offered.

"And you know that, how?" Agent Hailey retorted hotly. She glanced around with derision.

"I know that they seldom saw off the head, go through the brains looking for God Knows What, leave cigarette butts, beer cans, and what look to be donut sprinkles and footprints all around, make weird cuts all over her body with a knife and take the left nipple for a trophy. Oh. And by the way, she was raped."

"Shit! You're kidding."

"No. I'm not," said Leland. "Whoever is doing this, I doubt they're in it for the money. And as to whether they might have mob affiliations… Frankly, I don't think the mob would have anything to do with them.   You're looking at the ultimate loose cannon."

# The Feds Continued...

"What kind of cell is this?" Agent Hailey said, looking around. Leland wondered when they would remark on it.

Leland explained Ralph Bunch. Ralph Bunch was their local poet/painter /alcoholic who had been doing fine with a wife and kids until he got kicked in the head while milking his cow one day, which gave him blinding headaches he assuaged with drink. In time the headaches went away along with his wife and kids - but the drink stayed. The man was too proud to accept charity so when the cold came, Leland often had to arrest him - which actually was illegal. And in return Ralph painted murals to pay for his room and board, 'which probably was illegal too', Leland mused.

Just to see who had the better working knowledge of illegality in the area, Leland and Ruth, to pass the time would play the game, "So Arrest Me!" over lunch. They'd flip a coin to pick someone in the area. The first one to 'seize or detain something by legal authority', *'got their man'*. Nab a felon - and the other person bought lunch for a week. Leland had the upper hand in his understanding of the law. But Ruth was overwhelming with her knowledge of local affairs. Sometimes Leland wondered why he went driving around talking to people at all, instead of just sitting there chatting with Ruth.

But to get back to what we were talking about, Leland had Ruth run out for Ralph's paints and linseed oil. And while Ralph worked, the two of them would often chat - sometimes elaborating on a mental design for the perfect woman - to the strains of Chopin or Rossini with the odor of art in the air. It was a refreshing change from the boring smell of 'office'. And no one in Ralph's art work ever needed arresting, except perhaps for lewd conduct.

"That's his second wife." Leland pointed at the curvaceous nude with the red lips who was painted above the bunk they sat on, pink nipples fully aroused with the left having an enlarging pearly droplet of mother's milk hanging just above Agent Hailey's squinting right eyeball. 'Whom actually', Leland felt with absurd pride, 'he had

had a hand in designing.' Fronds and lovely moonlit flowers abounded. Strange animals filled the forest glade and strangely shaped clouds filled the ceiling sky. Leland smiled.

"How'd this *guy* find someone like *that* to marry him, after being kicked in the head and having his face rearranged by a cow?" Hailey frowned.

"He hasn't." Leland sighed. "This is just the schematic …for the model …for the prototype." Leland shook his head, and held up his palms at the futility of it all.

Hailey started to read some poetry scratched across the mons pubis.

"He's our local John LeClair." Leland shrugged.

Hailey raised her brows and gave Leland a second look. "He's not a suspect?"

"Hailey, you want to run across the way and get us some coffee?" Agent Curtis said.

"No," Agent Hailey said. But she rose slowly, and walked out swiftly, probably to best plan where she could linger to kick Agent Curtis in the nuts when *he* emerged.


Agent Curtis coughed. "You've been here ten years?"

Leland and Agent Curtis strolled back into his office. Ruth had found them a respectable chair, produced it, commanded them politely out of the jail cell, and shut the door, where she listened, catching what she could.

Where Agent Curtis had sent Agent Hailey, Ruth didn't know. But she would find that out soon enough too. She found out everything soon enough. That phone on her desk was like the center of a vast spider web. It rang with any little 'tingle' in the firmament.

"Actually, I grew up here," Leland said, staring out the window at Main Street, watching Agent Hailey stride across it. 'It was really wonderful how she managed that,' he mused.

Presently, the Press was right across the street drinking coffee in Mayor Pete's Campaign Café. Leland could see them looking through the window back at him looking through the window at them - and at Agent Hailey.

"I know." Agent Curtis nodded. "You played linebacker in high school. Attended Hanover State on scholarship where you majored in Criminal Law. And then worked another eight years for the LA Police Department, where you rose through the ranks, finally breaking your pick in the Latin Gangs division. Where, I imagine you may have picked up some Spanish.

"Si. Beuno. Sí, lo hice."

"I'll take that as a "yes"." Agent Curtis smiled. "…with qualifications."

"You'd be right." Leland was beginning to like him. "You're still not convinced Benny Green is not behind this, are you?" He said.

"No, I'm not."

"Why?"

"Benny isn't a complete fool. He reads the papers, and being a no-good, lo-life, dickhead, slime ball of a worthless pile of dog shit, he particularly *likes* the lurid crime stuff. He reads that there has just been a recent horrific murder, in Nancy Loomis' very area, committed by some kind of lunatic. People are worried it could the beginnings of a serial killer's rampage… and, Benny's sure of it! He got wind of what Nancy was doing with us, and this looks like a great way to tie up some loose ends."

"Yeah, I can see that." Leland nodded but privately felt this was garbage, and that this relaxed mano-mano charade had to end. People were getting killed out there and he had work to do. He rose. "Well, as long as you feel that way, I would guess that the resources of the Federal Government are with us?"

"That's pretty much the case," Agent Curtis agreed. "Until we have it confirmed, one way or the other."

"Good. Because I've got two bodies plus heads stacked up like cordwood over in the freezers at Vern Smithers' butcher shop, and enough evidence bagged in the back room by some local teenagers here to keep a small army of agents busy for at least a monht or so," Leland said.

"Okay." Agent Curtis stopped on his way to the door. "But tell me. I'm curious. How do you intend to proceed? I'm guessing you are still hanging onto your crazy lunatic, theory of events. But I would think in this isolated area, an oddball like this who suddenly appears would stick out like a sore thumb," Agent Curtis observed.

"Not really. The rural areas attract oddballs of every sort, plus drifters. There're a lot of itinerant farm laborers passing through. And then we've got a large Latino community."

"Your Spanish doesn't help you there?"

"I know the Latinos well enough around here that they'll tell me what they *can't* tell me, and that's pretty much everything. Something goes haywire in their community and they kick the guy across the boundary so's I can grab him. But otherwise it's a closed society. We probably have a thousand undocumented aliens working all around here whose bosses aren't particularly keen for them to be known, seen, or heard from. If this screwball has any kind of sense, all he has to do is put on about 2 extra shirts and a baseball cap and we'll be none the wiser. He could be walking past outside right now, or buying a gallon of milk and a six pack of beer down at the store."

As a matter of fact, Leland had just turned away from the front window and was shaking Agent Curtis' hand again, as Stan walked past... wearing two flannel shirts and a dirty Seattle Seahawks football cap.

# Romance Over Pie

Agent Hailey returned with two capped, Styrofoam containers of coffee.

"Where is Agent Curtis?" She looked around.

Leland nodded to indicate the direction Agent Curtis took.

Agent Hailey swore, stared up the street a while and then offered Leland the coffee.

"Thanks." He reached for the coffee. "Agent Curtis suggested I buy you a slice of cherry pie." He nodded his head to indicate the café across the street out of which she had just come.

"So he pimped me out again." Agent Hailey snorted. She took a moment to survey her options, which included a short visual inspection of Leland. "Sure."

Leland glanced both ways and made to lead across the street. Agent Hailey paused. "All those press boys are inside you know."

"I know," Leland called from mid-street. "Ruth hates having them underfoot and milling around outside. So she promised them updates if they'd wait in the café." Leland nodded across the street. "Seems to be working so far."

Agent Hailey furrowed her brows and followed.

Inside Carmella ushered them to Leland's regular booth. It was at the far end nearby the juke box. Whenever Leland wished to have an especially private conversation he pushed in a quarter and played "Rock Around the Clock".

"How's business Carmella?"

"Not bad. The press corps, they are pretty cheap. But there's a lot of them. And if you keep them waiting long enough they're going to buy a meal."

"I'll see what I can do." Leland smiled.

"Thank you," Carmella said. "You might also suggest to them that a tip would help to lubricate your lips."

Leland smiled. "I'll do what I can Carmella."

Carmella nodded down the way towards the boy sitting at the counter working on what looked to be the second of two huge floats. "That's the one pulling in the chips. He offers to take them to the scenes of the crimes. He charges thirty dollars a trip, I've heard. And he will only take one person at a time. My guess is, he's making more than you." Carmella nodded, as she flipped the page on her waitress pad. "What will you have?"

Leland recognized the boy who had run the Mercedes.

"Two pieces of your cherry pie. And maybe these coffees in some cups?" Leland handed Carmella the Styrofoam containers.

Carmella scribbled. "Sure," she said, leaving.

Leland stared out the café window, in order to keep from staring at certain parts of Agent Hailey, which actually he could observe well enough in the reflection of the window.

"Agent Curtis does this all the time, you know."

Her voice seemed to be saying "look at me". So Leland did. Really nice breasts, bound really tight, beneath a buttoned up blouse. If she'd just worn a normal shirt it wouldn't have been as near as much of a turn on. But the manner in which she had tried to conceal her sexuality was tormenting it and making it scream. Any guy would want to help. Plus she was very good looking with plush lips, a proud nose, pale freckles, and a glance like tropical beach water. Leland just could not take his eyes off her. Coming over to Pete's café had never gotten him this excited.

"He pretends to drive off without me. I get invited for pie. We chat. I learn all I can. He says it's just a matter of utilizing all of our assets. That I should do the same thing for him - if it's a younger woman."

"It will be a struggle to give fair value." Leland smiled.

"You don't mind being used?"

"Use away."

Agent Hailey shrugged. "Fine then."

The pie came.

"It's pretty good pie here."

"Good," Agent Hailey barked.

Carmella set it with a conspiratorial smile, and left. The first reporter approached.

"Sheriff. Vince Delaney of the Seattle Times. Do you have an I D on the second victim yet?"

"Yes we do."

With that the rest of the press rose. Leland raised a palm and turned his attention so all could hear.

"My advice: Order yourself a nice meal. Tip the waitress generously. Maybe get a drink. And if you just wait until I'm done conferring with my colleague here, I'll tell you more."

The man from the Times was about to open his mouth when Leland shook his head and rotated his index finger back towards the group. The man's mouth closed, and he turned back to rejoin the group.

"So! What can I get for you all?" Carmella cried.

Agent Hailey and Leland continued their conversation.

"I don't know when I've been so closely observed," Agent Hailey said uncomfortably.

"Sorry," Leland said.

"I don't mean you. I meant *them*." She turned her head. Leland nodded.

"When it comes time, would you like to say a few words also?"

Agent Hailey's lovely lips parted. "Uh... no?"

"A large part of advancing in the law game involves public speaking."

"No. I'd rather you just go ahead and advance yourself. I'll just concentrate upon catching a killer."

"Alright."

They ate their pie quietly. Agent Hailey raised her head to speak, perhaps to apologize, but Leland shook his. "Save it," he said. The last thing he needed now was an argument with a woman. Especially a beautiful one. Nothing more depressing than being unlikeable to a woman that beautiful. His ego was still in the shop from his last.

Once Leland had seen that all the reporters were starting to tuck themselves into their meals, he pushed himself back from the table and rose, mouthing sotto voce, "It's time for the Kimmel County Dinner Theater."

Agent Hailey's eyes followed him as he made his way over to the press corps and pulled out a chair which he leaned over the back of. "I'm Leland Kelly, Sheriff of Kimmel County, for those of you who don't know me. And I appreciate you saving your questions for the present time. This is Agent Hailey of the Federal Bureau of Investigation." A lot of the men craned their necks for a better look, as their brows rose. Several diners who were not members of the press contingent nodded quietly also, damping the clatter of their cutlery as they followed developments with gawking gazes. "The Bureau has generously offered its help, both manpower and technical acumen, to Kimmel County in a combined effort to track the perpetrator of these egregious crimes. Though we have not yet identified the identity of the first victim, the second victim appears to be a middle-aged woman from the Seattle area by the name of Nancy Loomis."

A hush fell over the press crowd. "You mean… the Muffin Lady?!" a voice cried out.

Leland nodded. "Apparently she is also popularly known as the Muffin Lady."

The Muffin Lady was a well known figure in the area, having been spotlighted in many promotional ads for her company.

"Was she decapitated like the first victim?" A reporter cried out.

Leland paused, considering how much he wanted to reveal, and was beginning to shake his head, when a teenager in braids, from over her writing pad, declared: "Something was rolling around in that body bag like a bowling ball."

Leland looked directly at Nancy Gillis, who had poked her head out from behind the reporter from the Seattle Times. All heads turned to Nancy Gillis. "You were at the scene initially?" One of the reporters asked.

"Yes she was," Leland answered, in an effort to take charge of the briefing once again. "And the victim *was* decapitated. Though whether this confirms linkage with the first victim is still to be determined."

The reporters were now turned to Nancy Gillis and tossing her questions. She was quite demur with her answers, and ended it finally by saying, "All of your questions will soon be answered in the next issue of the Kimmel High School's Wolverine News due out tomorrow! I suggest you get an issue! We're starting with a three part series. The first portion will begin with an evaluation of the scene of the crime. The second will involve a short interview, conducted directly thereafter, with the lead investigator, Kimmel County Sheriff Leland Kelly." She nodded to include Leland. "And the third, which I am still working on, will cover the extent and reason for possible Federal involvement in the case. As for local color and the reaction from local residents, we have made an executive decision to let this softer news be covered by the more standard commercial news outlets." The press corps blank looks said a lot. "That's it for now! If you need me for any further comment, I can be reached through the Wolverine Press." Nancy Gillis finished quickly, and then she left.

Leland waited and then tried beginning his briefing anew: "As I was saying…"

But everyone was watching Nancy Gillis' exit from the café - then hop on a bike and pedal away.

"Who is that?" The first reporter to look back at Leland asked.

# Rape Kit

After Leland had dealt with the last of the reporters, he settled himself in the booth where he returned to eating his pie across from Agent Hailey.

"You want to come with me to visit a suspect?" He asked.

"Why all the favors?" Agent Hailey replied.

"As long as you're going to get pimped, you might as well get paid." Leland said. "Besides you may come in handy."

"Handy? How so?" Agent Hailey put down her fork. She hadn't eaten much of the pie. Which was too bad, Leland thought, because the pie was good. "You want the rest of it?" She asked.

Leland rose. "C'mon, let's go."

As they left the café Leland shouted back to Carmella, "Department billing."

Carmella flipped her receipt book and wrote this on the back of the check.

"Regular tip," Leland added.

Carmella nodded and scribbled a quick calculation on the front of the check. "What do you want me to call it?!" Carmella called after him. "Departmental outreach?" "Community relations?" She flipped the receipt book over again as she smiled at Leland.

Leland slammed the door behind him.

Out by the Kimmel County Sheriff's SUV, Leland paused before unlocking the vehicle. "If you come, you've got to promise me this is just between you and me. The FBI proper needn't know any of this yet."

Agent Hailey didn't hop in.

"Hey. They 'pimp' you out. They're assuming you'll do what's needed to please the customer."

Agent Hailey looked up and down the street, perhaps looking for her vanished partner as she considered this.

"Why don't you want me to share any of this with the Agency?" Agent Hailey asked, after she'd settled in and fastened her seat belt.

"Because this town only has one dentist. And if the FBI were to interrogate him presently, like as not, he'd be whisked off to a black project somewhere and we'd never see him again." Leland pulled down his lower lip. "And I've got receding gums."

"Sorry to hear that," Agent Hailey replied.

Leland nodded.

Leland left out town by a network of back alleys and crossing a dirt lot or two. Agent Hailey gripped the door handle as if this Sheriff were the town lunatic. But when Leland indicated the rear view mirror with a nod of his head, Agent Hailey understood. Leland had shaken the press corps. The last of the press vehicles was bottomed out on a log hidden in a field of weeds. The fellow was getting out slowly to inspect the damage.

"So…" Leland began as they hit the paved road leading north out of town with a brief chirp of the tires. "…Ramey, our local dentist / psychic." He began filling Agent Hailey in on the details to date as he drove swiftly north.

By the time they had reached Ramey's, Agent Hailey was pretty well up to speed on all that Leland presently knew about the case - as it applied to Ramey.

"It sounds to me like we have already located the killer," Agent Hailey said as they pulled into Ramey's gravel drive. There was another car there, which Leland knew to be Doctor Chatham's. "Unless you believe this man can truly predict events?" Agent Hailey adjusted her hip holster to cant her duty weapon a bit more comfortably. The Glock 23 functioned flawlessly in sand, rain, and mud, but carried like a plastic brick.

"Were it so simple," Leland sighed. He remained seated in the car and indicated Agent Hailey should do likewise. "There are ways any normal person, and especially a hypersensitive dentist/psychic like Ramey could have come across a snippet of this information around here. And then there are some other discrepancies. Ramey doesn't have any buddies to speak of, and all indications are that

43

these crimes involve two perps. Second, I know that Ramey is nervous around any kind of weapon. And third, I just have a real hard time imagining Ramey as any kind of sadistic murderer." Leland indicated Agent Hailey's revolver. "So let's not shoot him, just yet."

"Fine," Agent Hailey said, holstering her revolver. "Do I take the front or the back?"

"You take the side," Leland indicated with a toss of his head. "That way you'll be able to see both exits. I'll go in. Give me five minutes. And I'll either step back out and wave you in, or you can break down the door and come in shooting."

"Gee. Sounds like fun."

So that's what they did. Agent Hailey stationed herself twenty yards south of the house, where she could see both entrances to the home with revolver raised and locked in both hands. And Leland rang the buzzer.

Doctor Chatham answered it, peering out the cracked door. Leland had to bend down to hear him.

"He wants a rape kit," Doctor Chatham said in his elderly voice.

"You're kidding," Leland replied.

"Noooope!"

# Rape Kit Continued

"*And...*" Doctor Chatham's hand came out of the door pushing Sheriff Leland back, "he wants a woman." The fingers extended holding Leland back further. "...and not Ruth."

Leland stood there nonplussed.

"I believe it is in the patient's best interest, Leland," Doc Chatham whispered.

"And I believe I've got just what you need." Leland holstered his pistol.

He waved Agent Hailey over. By the time she had stepped up to the door, Ramey's curious face appeared.

"Ramey, meet Agent Hailey of the FBI. Agent Hailey, of the FBI, meet Ramey."

Leland pushed on the door.

"Ramey. You're going to have to open the door *wider* if you want to Agent Hailey to be able to get through."

The door opened wider.

Ramey's living area was unusually disordered and in twilight. Newspapers had been flung about. There were several open wine bottles and quite a few dead beers. Glasses were here and there. The far side of the living area looked like it had had a fist punched through the wall board.

Leland introduced Agent Hailey again with a nod.

Ramey looked terrible, but he sized Agent Hailey up with a hardened look that Leland had never seen on the dentist before. Ramey let the door swing open as he turned on his heel and stepped back inside. Agent Hailey cast Leland a questioning look.

He motioned that she should go in.

"I'll get the kit," Leland said.


"It's not so much a split-personality disorder as it is a two-person personality disorder," Dr. Chatham said as he conferred

45

quietly with Leland outside on some porch chairs.

Meanwhile, Agent Hailey was inside questioning Ramey and performing a rape kit exam, 'however *that* goes,' Leland wondered.

"Typically, with a split personality, it's just that." Doc Chatham stared at Leland intently. "Each of the personalities may have their own name because they share none of the personality traits of the other. Whichever character represents the splinter personality is what the literary crowd might call a 'stock' character or a 'flat' character. They are the simple possessor of one character trait the heretofore 'whole' personality disavows, in essence saying, 'that's not me.'" Doc Chatham spread his arms wide. "Like Doris and ...Jezebelle!"

Leland nodded. He'd watched the movies too. And he didn't much care for this 'psychobabble'.

"But in Ramey's case, this 'splinter personality' is much more like a 'whole' person! It has its own name, sure. But it also has a history and knows things which would seemingly be foreign to a person like Ramey. Unless our Ramey has been *very* clever at living two, totally different lives of which *one* life is as a *woman*." Doc Chatham stopped as if to let that sink in. "I have never heard of a personality splitting into someone of the opposite sex." He paused. "Who, is actually quite successful - to hear her tell it."

Leland wondered how old Doc Chatham thought this was going to play here in Kimmel County. Then, Leland calculated the doctor's age and figured his psychiatric training was probably taken when Freud was still in vogue.

"The upshot of this is that either I am being totally buffaloed, or I've never seen or heard of anything of this sort before."

Leland stared at him.

"That is, of course, outside of the movies."

"Oh yeah? What movies have you seen?"

"I was just being rhetorical... or something," Doc Chatham spread his hands... possibly in hope. As if he were entreating Leland to dispel the confusion and perhaps come up with something. But Leland wasn't in a helpful mood.

"Fine. Okay. Thanks for your help in this time of crisis Doc," Leland grumbled.

This got old Doc Chatham's back up. "You can discuss the fee with my office manager, Leland." The Doc rose stiffly and left. Leland didn't want to take up *anything* with *her*. And he didn't think Ruth would either.

Leland stood outside for a while, before he figured it was better that he go in. 'Just 'cause it was silent, you never knew what could have happened', he considered. He knocked softly.

"C'mon in," Agent Hailey chirruped sweetly. "We're all done." She opened the door with an elbow while snapping a latex glove from her right hand.

Ramey was lying naked on a living room table partially covered by a sheet with his knees up, casting an imploring glance at the Sheriff.

"You don't want to know," Agent Hailey said, in answer to Leland's astonished glance.

# Ramey Gets Interrogated

Ramey had emptied two bottles of wine getting through the rape kit procedure and was now fast asleep under the sheet, his breathing ragged with glottal stops and gasps, a jerk, and then his head lolling off the table top. He'd then awake abruptly, only to readjust and resume his stupor. It was annoying. And it was interrupting Leland's conversation with Agent Hailey. Leland shoved Ramey's head roughly back onto the table for the umpteenth time. "Shut up Ramey," Leland said.

Ramey murmured something dental and vaguely menacing, took a lazy swat at the air, missing Leland by a foot, and rolled over.

"I scraped his nails, took a buccal swab, and checked him for cuts and bruises, scratches, the works. He's clean as a baby's butt and with hands just about as soft," Agent Hailey said. "It makes no sense.

Leland snapped himself from his reverie. He might have been waiting for her eyes to twinkle. The woman was just so damned beautiful he felt as if he were watching a movie. "It does if he's just a dentist," Leland said.

Agent Hailey moved them quietly out of Ramey's hearing. 'All they needed was soft lamp lit fog, the steam from a locomotive's brakes releasing, and just time enough to confess his thoughts,' Leland thought sadly, with the regrets of someone who feels he is going to miss that train.

Agent Hailey frowned. "Usually there's a telltale. You don't just drag a struggling woman 30 yards through undergrowth, in the dark, to a spot where she's beaten and raped after meanwhile taking several shots at you, without some kind of abrasive evidence. It doesn't add up. Even the most careful killers usually have some kind of scratch to explain away, or forest dirt under their nails, or hair or blood splatters, or knuckle abrasions, or clothes to dispose of. It just doesn't make sense."

"*Unless* he's the mild-mannered dentist who didn't do it."

"How could he have known all of this beforehand, if he didn't do it?"

"He didn't know all of it beforehand. He just knew her name."

"Then how could he have known her name."

"I don't know. Maybe he overheard it from some gassed patient blathering on under the effects of an anesthetic which stimulated his already overly excitable imagination," Sheriff Leland got a little excited himself, "… into a formed narrative of great moment?" Leland smiled. Agent Hailey looked at him funny.

"Then how could he know all of it *afterward*?" Agent Hailey pursed her lips, leaning in.

"*Less* impossible…"

"Not much."

Leland paused before answering. Agent Hailey was actually hissing softly as she decompressed. But the difference between hissing and puckering for a kiss was spatially pretty much similar. Leland imagined angling his head this way and that, considering which attitude most got their noses out of the way. It was mostly a matter of attitude, Leland considered… and remained lost in these considerations until she kicked him.

He rubbed his shin. "Kicking me doesn't make me any smarter."

Agent Hailey smiled knowingly. "You talk to the guy a while, while I go through the house."

"We haven't a warrant."

"*You* haven't a warrant. He signed one for me." Agent Hailey gave a pert flip of her head. "Actually, *she* signed one for me. But I'm thinking it's probably valid, given the circumstances."

Leland waved her off. Agent Hailey was *really* interfering with his focus. And he figured it was about time to interrogate Ramey, anyway.

"So. Ramey," Leland called out to the bleary dentist after he had rousted him and administered some strong, hot coffee. "What's been going on with you?"

"Oh, Leland. You wouldn't believe…" Ramey's head snapped back and a sharp, crisp demanding woman's voice issued from the other side of his mouth. "Have you caught my rapist yet?"

Leland was caught aback. Ramey's whole aspect changed. He looked mad as a wet hen. Which was it exactly. Not a wet rooster. A wet hen.

Leland thought it best to begin with the more reasonable of the two, and the one he had a friendship with. Leland tried to speak as obligingly as was possible. "Ma'am, I realize you probably have a lot you will want to tell me, but I would like to speak with Ramey, the *dentist*, first."

"*He* wasn't raped."

Leland next expected Ramey's head to turn entirely around while vomiting green goo. But as nothing of the sort happened, he remained firm. "The *dentist*, please."

Ramey's head snapped back, and it was Ramey the original. "Oh, Leland," Ramey began again. "I feel as if I'm married, only I'm 25 years in and we're really getting on each other's nerves. She won't leave me alone! She wants this done. She wants that done. Nothing's quite right. She just doesn't seem to be able to be satisfied. And she's got all this *anger*, which I feel she projects onto me. Who I feel she doesn't *really* know, or actually *care* to know. I finally had to give up and started drinking. How do married men take it?"

"I don't know, Ramey. I'm not married."

Ramey nodded. "Why do men ever enter into such a state?" Ramey whined.

"I don't know, Ramey. I think maybe sex has a lot to do with it." Leland put his hand on Ramey's shoulder. "At least, it seems responsible for a lot of the crazy things I see in my line of work."

"Yeah." Ramey nodded.

"Look, Ramey. I'm sorry I didn't get back to you sooner. Okay?"

Ramey rolled his eyes.

"But I need to know. What is this thing between you and Nancy Loomis? How are you two connected? How did you know she was going to get murdered?"

"I *didn't* know she was going to be murdered, Leland. All I was doing was mowing my yard! Even now. You see how it's half done. Did you even *notice* the mower left out there? I was *mowing my yard* when suddenly, I received these horrific visions, and the name "Nancy Loomis" sounded in my ears. You remember when I realized your 13 year old cat, Lucy, had been hit and killed, and then drug off into the woods by a coyote, and I knew just where to find her?" Leland nodded. "It was just like that. So I called Ruth - who was as officious as ever. Leland, I have to say, that woman is not to be trusted with power. Do you know she calls your Sheriff's office a department - no that's not it. ...a *bureau*, when you aren't listening?"

"Yes, I know this Ramey."

"Well, anyway. So I'm trying to tell her what I know, but I need to know *what* I know for certain before I commit myself because, as you know, in these small towns it's very *hard* to preserve your reputation as a professional. You've just got to watch it like a hawk! So I try to ask Ruth what she knows about a 'Nancy Loomis'. But she says she can't reveal any information about an ongoing investigation. So I say, "So there is an ongoing investigation regarding Nancy Loomis?" To which she says, "I can't say. We can't reveal information regarding any ongoing investigation either factual or fantastical". You know how bureaucrats talk and repeat the same things with that kind of nasal thing going when they're trying to disdain you? Well, Ruth *does* that, Leland."

"I know, Ramey."

"And then pretends like she doesn't know me. I'm her *dentist*, for Pete's sake Leland."

"I know, Ramey. I know."

Ramey sighed. "So I tell her to have you call me. And of course you *don't* call me. And the rest is history."

"I'll say I'm sorry one more time, Ramey, and then that's it."

Ramey nodded.

"You haven't taken me up to the part where you got married."

"Married? Oh yeah." Ramey shook his head, *rattled* it, actually. "There wasn't much to it. I go to bed. And the next thing I know, I wake up. And there's this partly naked woman in a ruined dress in my head with me. I mean, she's a mess! And she's pissed as hell. It's like one of those Las Vegas wedding things I'd guess, where you head out drinking, and the next thing you know you're waking up in some strange motel room with some woman you don't recognize - who smiles at you with just these *awful* teeth - who says you're married. I mean, it's a mind blower Leland. And you're left just casting about for landmarks. Which, again, is why I called you."

"I know. I know. And I'm sorry, Ramey. But I'm here now."

"Yeah."

"Look. Maybe it's time I speak with Nancy..."

"It's Ms. Loomis to *us* Leland. And I think that's a good idea. And while you're at it, could you just tell her that I didn't have anything to do with whatever has happened to her, and so perhaps she could just calm down a little, at least with me? It's a *very* small space in here. I mean, inside my head."

"I'll do what I can Ramey."

"Thanks." Ramey's head turned, and the fish wife re-appeared. "That took you long enough."

"Well," Leland said, "Ramey had some concerns."

"He's a fucking *dentist*. Who *cares* what concerns a fucking *dentist* has?"

"Well, to a "fucking dentist", strange as it may seem, *their* concerns sometimes reign uppermost, in *their* minds."

"Well they shouldn't. Because, God knows, I've been complaining loud enough."

"He agrees, which gets us to something he wanted me to bring up with you."

"I'm in his *own head*, and he needs an intermediary?"

"Well, perhaps you come on a little strong."

"It's a *man's world*! How would you expect me to come on? Do you know how hard it is for a woman to make a go of it in the kind of 'Good 'Ol Boy' business climate there is that exists out there? Do you think I just got given a 5 million dollar industry to run? No! I didn't think so. I had to build it from scratch. From the mixing bowl up! And after all that, all that toil and sweat and after breaking the glass ceiling all on my own without any help from you or any other *man*, do you know they call me? The *Muffin Lady*. Well, you know what? I wear that moniker as a badge of pride. Go ahead. Call me the Muffin Lady. And I'll call you and raise you 5 million dollars. What do you think of that?"

"I think that you've shown a lot of pluck."

"Luck? Luck?! What's luck got to do with it?"

"I said, pluck... PLUCK!"

"Okay. Well, good then. He must have messed up my hearing when he punched me in my good ear."

"That's probably it. Now if we could just get to your recounting of events?"

"I would *love* to go there, finally, for Christ's sake." A tear trickled down Ramey's cheek. "You're going to help me nail this bastard?" Leland felt some sympathy rise up. He patted his gun.

"I'm going to blow a big wide hole, right through him."

"That sounds good. That works for me."

Leland nodded, and they began their interrogation.

# Ramey Goes to Jail

Leland and Agent Hailey conferred while Ramey lay down with a cold compress on his forehead. Agent Hailey found nothing incriminating in Ramey's home following a thorough search… no blood staining clothing, no mud stained boots. Nothing out of the ordinary in fact except some rather technical books covering dental technique with some full color plates of some dental maladies which could make your skin crawl. And Ms. Loomis' questioning had produced remarkably similar accounts of the crime, with a similar timeline of events. There were clearly two men involved, one of whom was clearly the follower. And it being pitch black out that night, Nancy Loomis could identify neither except by their voices.

"So what are you planning to do with him?" Agent Hailey asked.

"Well, I thought I'd talk to Ramey about it," Leland replied.

"Well why not," Agent Hailey growled rhetorically. "In the big city we *arrest* murderers, but wouldn't it be nice to try to reach an amicable settlement." She smiled.

"You have a nice smile," Leland said.

"This is not my *nice* smile," Agent Hailey responded.

"Ramey!" Leland hoisted up his trousers and shouted some to get Ramey's attention. "What do you want to do?"

Ramey looked as baffled as Agent Hailey. So Leland explained.

"On the one hand, there is no way Agent Hailey here feels that you cannot be a *prime suspect* in this brutal and cruel crime. So if we go with her estimate of events, you should be arrested." Leland said with a tilt of his head towards Agent Hailey. "Maybe even roughed up a bit …trying to escape and all that."

Agent Hailey returned Ramey a blank stare.

Ramey looked distressed.

"However," Leland continued, gripping Ramey on the shoulder, "my hunch tells me that you are innocent."

Ramey raised his finger to agree, "Oh, thank you Leland!" and to possibly add something...

"..And that there is something going on here that while on the surface of things looks to be quite strange - as events unfold and we put the pieces together differently, we *could* conceivably find your heretofore fantastic story to be entirely credible and understandable... perhaps even overstated."

"And *how*... in what *parallel dimension*, would the pieces ever line up that way?" Agent Hailey asked.

Ramey raised a hand to comment again. But Agent Hailey's glare intimidated him, and Leland continued.

"However, if I were to let you walk around here free as a bird, things being as they are, rumors could start about me or about you... all questioning my good sense or your innocence... Then, an angry mob forms, or the killer might try to silence you himself, seeing as how you harbor the only partially living witness to the crime."

"An angry mob? You think the killer would try to kill *me*?" Ramey squeaked. "But, that... ...but he's supposed to kill women!" Ramey nodded at Agent Hailey.

"To get to her, he has to go through you," Leland replied.

"Oh my Lord." Ramey started hyperventilating. Agent Hailey gave him an latex glove to breath into.

"So, in which case, it would seem our best move would be to put you in protective custody," Leland spoke sympathetically.

Agent Hailey shook her head. The glove was growing pretty big.

"Which way would you like to go?"

The latex gloves' thumbs pointed upwards. "You would like protective custody?"

Ramey nodded between breaths.

"Protective custody it is then." Leland smiled at Agent Hailey.

Agent Hailey frowned.

Then they set about collecting a few of Ramey's personal items for the trip into town.

# Whiteboard

A week passed. They had identified the first murder victim as Clarisse Clemens, another newbie to the area. Which explained why no one had appeared to claim her body (parts). Also, she had a rap sheet. Apparently at one time she had worked as a prostitute and a bunko artist. Neither one very successfully as it appeared, because she was found way out here and missing her head with only a total of $19.37 and a six pack of condoms in her pocketbook. Agent Hailey had retrieved a lot more information about her from their forensics team, which Agent Curtis wanted her to postpone sharing until *he* could be present. Presently he was in the city preparing to move against Benny Green and his operation, and he wanted to keep his 'operational status' clear. Not entangled in that 'rural muck' portion of the investigation. "Besides," he said over the phone, "that's why Agent Hailey is there. I assume you two are working together okay?"

"Yes, we're fine," Leland replied. "She's very capable. There's no need to rush for that reason. Although I would like a look at those findings as soon as possible, the pressure in a small community to find the perpetrator being what it is," Leland said.

"I'll be there as soon as I can," Agent Curtis replied curtly. "But just so you know, Benny Green is still my top suspect."

"We'll see you when you get here," Leland replied and hung up.

"You've got all the forensics sent?" Leland asked.

"Faxed this morning," Agent Hailey replied.

"Thanks," Leland replied. If Agent Curtis knew the kind of end run Agent Hailey and he were perpetrating, he might have to re-consider who was pimping who. As it stood now, Leland had an inside to the full resources of the FBI through Agent Hailey. And Agent Hailey had a full run of the investigation through him. And 'all there is left now is marriage!' Leland made a joke with himself. He smiled, happily.

Agent Hailey had softened quite a bit under Leland's

professional wooing and was becoming a real part of the team '…of two', Leland considered happily.  Another day with his dream law enforcer.  He had never been so happy chasing a murderer.

Agent Hailey was examining him oddly.

"Maybe we'd ought to go over that new evidence again and tape it up," Leland said.

In addition to the whiteboard, Agent Hailey had brought some yarn and marking pens… for doing some mind mapping of the crime on the far wall.  Ruth was impressed.  "Never saw me do this to chase down a missing cow, now did you?"  Leland grinned.

Ruth smiled.  Ruth was happy when Sheriff Leland was happy. And currently, he was chasing down this cruel, ruthless, absolutely amoral serial murderer as if he were two feet in the air like a love struck schoolboy.  Ruth just hoped he didn't become too addled by infatuation.  This guy, whoever he was, was a stone-cold killer.  And about Agent Hailey, she still hadn't made up her mind.

"You see this latest news?  It's that 'in-depth' interview that schoolgirl Nancy Gillis did of you coming back on the bus from the crime scene and written up for the Kimmel High Wolverine."  Ruth dropped a newspaper upon Leland's desk.

It hit with quite a thud!

Leland's mind was on the whiteboard, but he turned when he heard the paper hit.  "The Kimmel County Wolverine sells that much advertising?"  Leland asked, turning to the stack of newsprint.

Ruth shook her head.  "It's the *New York Times,*" Ruth said deadpan.

Leland and Agent Hailey both stared as Ruth turned the front page of the New York Times to where they could see the picture and headline just below the fold.

The dramatic black and white photo was of  "Sheriff Leland Kelly, Kimmel County Sheriff, oiling and reassembling his 45 caliber Colt Anaconda behind the partly open blinds of his front office."

The headline read:

# "THEY PURSUE SERIAL KILLERS DIFFERENTLY IN KIMMEL COUNTY"

Ruth gave Leland the sober eye.

"Oh Lord," Leland whispered.

# Meanwhile, Back on the Farm

Harriet was a pretty quick study. A woman had to be when she was hefty and plain of appearance. And she figured this Stan fellow was a real 'misogynist' the minute she saw him... which didn't bother her none, or much, anyway. She figured all men were, and to tell you the truth, she wasn't all that impressed with women folk herself. She didn't hold it against the men much for not finding her attractive. Hell, it wasn't their fault. But it did gall her when the women would slight her for the same thing. Now, *that* was just downright mean. It was like someone crossing the street just to stand in your way.

"You don't like women much do you?" Harriet said to the hired man, Stan, as she set the evening's mashed spuds on the table.

"Now why would you say that?" Stan took this quite seriously. Harriet liked that.

Her husband, Bob, on the other hand, visibly stiffened. He was such a puppy.

"You look to be about 30-35 maybe, passable looking, and you're still single, or at least runnin' around all by yourself and not fittin' in exactly anywheres."

"Maybe I like them, but they don't like me."

Harriet noticed Bob's smile as he said this.

"I'd believe that," Harriet said.

Bob thought Harriet had been suspicious ever since they came back that morning with blood all over themselves and complaining about a "triple-breeched stillbirth" over at the Munson's spread. (Stan had warned him not to make such an extravagant story of it.) Bob became pretty certain as the meals began deteriorating. But he wasn't certain, certain until Harriet pulled the gun on Stan.

Here they were chowing down! Bob had been in a pretty good mood despite Harriet's glowering. He felt like he had gotten all flushed out down below and was just about ready for more. The prices for milk were good. The cows were healthy. The pastures were all dry for the season. And it had been a warm Sunday! So all in all, it seemed a shame when Harriet pulled out that gun and aimed it at Stan, one of the best hands they'd ever had.

"I want you outta here," she said.

"You want to talk privately with your husband?" Stan inquired, calm as could be. Bob just couldn't help but admire this.

"No. I don't want to talk privately with that adulterer!"

"I ain't no adulterer."

"You had sex outside the bounds of marriage, didn't ya?" Harriet turned the gun on Bob.

"Woman, what are you talking about?" Bob flushed.

"I'm talking about putting your wee little pecker into someone, somewhere where's you shouldn't. An' now about you bein' a bald faced liar to boot." Harriet reached down and pulled out the Sunday edition of the New York Times which she slammed down on the supper table.

Bob looked dumbly at it as if he were staring at an old school textbook of the advanced sort.

"Turn it over. It's below the fold." Harriet nudged the newspaper forward with the barrel of the gun.

"Below the fold?"

"Look at the other side!"

"On the bottom of the page," Stan advised.

"That's right," Harriet said.

Bob turned the damned heavy newspaper over, and a trickle of fear crawled up his back leg like a bug. There was a headline about Sheriff Leland and Serial Killers. Bob turned his wide eyes on Stan without thinking. Then he pulled his gaze back. "I don't see anything in here about adultery. Mine, or anyone else's," Bob said.

"I believe they call it "rape"." Harriet lifted the tip of her gun to emphasize the point.

"How the hell would they know that the rapist is a married man, Harriet?" Bob indicated. "There's no way. That's the answer."

"They don't say it's a married man, you blinkin' idiot!"

"Well then, I don't see how you can come off callin' it an adultery!" Bob matched her volume.

"*I'm* callin' it an adultery, because *I* think that you and Stan here did it." Harriet moved the barrel of the gun so that it was pointed midway in between the both of them.

Bob said nothing, because he couldn't think for a moment what he should say. And then, when he finally decided he should say "No", to deny it, Stan was already talking.

"You sure are a good cook, Harriet," Stan said. "You mind if I continue eating?" He nodded at the gun.

"Just keep your hands where I can see them," Harriet said. "An' don't take more than two pork chops."

Stan nodded and continued eating. He did it with such a relish, he was actually making Bob hungry to watch. Which was something, considering a cold wave of fear had just about frozen Bob to his chair and shriveled his genitals into small hard nuts and squirreled them high up into his scrotum. He was either going to get shot, or going to admit something he'd rather not. Either choice was rather riveting. And Bob couldn't see how Stan was able to take it all so lightly. "Maybe you could tell Harriet where we wuz, Stan," Bob entreated. "Seeing as how you've got a better head for explanations and such." Bob nodded.

The only thing Bob could figure was that Stan must know something he did not. Which must be why he was taking all of this so cool.

"We wuz wherever you two ends up figuring we wuz, I'd guess. You're the boss." Stan smiled, chewing.

"What the hell. Why are you saying that?!" Bob exclaimed.

"Well. Where 'wuz' we?" Stan asked.

Bob was totally flummoxed.

"Yeah, then. Where wuz you?" Harriet aimed the gun at Bob.

"Well. What? I don't know. I mean, when? When are you talkin' about? Wuz it then, or last night or two weeks ago. What are you talkin' about?"

"Ah'm talkin' about *when* Ms. Muffin Lady here got clobbered." Harriet thumped the newspaper with the barrel of the gun. "Where wuz you then? That night?"

"Honey. I can't remember where I am every night of the year."

"Ah'm not askin' about every night of the year. Ah'm just asking about them as when you're not in bed at home asleep where you oughta be."

"Well, them too. Those are hard to keep track of. I mean, there's cows that need milkin', dogs that start barking all hours of the night. You *know* how crazy it can get around here!"

"I'd think you'd remember if you was off rapin' some woman, and draggin' her in the darkness from some car on the highway." Harriet nodded.

"It's the kind of thing that would stick in my mind, that is, as an employee." Stan nodded, as he relished another bite.

"And I don't know what you're laughin' about either. As I'm just a split second away from shootin' you too." Harriet eyeballed Stan.

"Why aren't you helpin' me deny all this?" Bob whined. "I thought we wuz partners. I thought we wuz together on this."

"So you're admittin' everything?"

"Ah'm not admittin' anything, woman," Bob declared hotly. "An' just cause you got a gun doesn't make no difference either."

"You might feel a bit different once I use it." Harriet's finger clenched tightly on the trigger.

Stan put down his knife and fork and raised his hands.

Both Harriet and Bob looked at him.

"Harriet. You start out pointing the gun at me, but if this keeps on you're going to end up shooting your only husband, Bob," Stan pointed out. He paused to push his plate away, take out a cigarette and light it - all the while keeping his hands plainly visible. He inhaled, then exhaled up towards the bare light bulb. Bob just had to admire this no end, in spite of the dire situation. And he did

62

appreciate the help, a bit.

"Don't you just admire that?" Bob gestured to Harriet. "Can't you admire that? I mean, look. You're got a gun pointed at the man. An' rather than getting' all upset an' cryin' an' whimperin', or yellin', like you'd half expect, he's just cool as a cucumber and sets there ready to discuss things." Bob waved his finger between himself and Harriet. "*We* could take a lesson there."

"An' you could take a bullet here." Harriet scowled, poking the gun at Bob's pecker.

"Stan," Bob said. "I appreciate your cool and all that, but I think right now it's best if we explain to Harriet just wut it is we got to say."

Harriet moved the gun sights back on Stan. "An *I think* it's best he don't provoke me."

Stan shrugged. He looked at Bob.

"All I'm saying dear," Bob tried to continue as best he could in as soothing voice as he could, ""…instead of getting all upset about some Muffin Lady who gets herself killed an' probably nothin' more than she deserved, in some New York newspaper there…" Bob pointed, "…is that perhaps you don't recognize a quality man. I mean, here is a quality man. He works hard. He works smart. And he's cool as a cucumber under any kind of trouble, and here you want to go runnin' him off with a gun?!"

"Ah may just shoot 'im, and drag him off with a back hoe," Harriet spit.

"Well that's yur *problem*. You just don't recognize *quality*. You just don't and never did!" Bob was getting upset, gun or no. "Now I know for a fact that there may have been other crime figures involved! Now wasn't she saying somethin' about thinkin' we were in with Benny Green, or somebody?!"

Stan sighed.

Harriet just shook her head.

Bob considered a moment. "…oops."

"You see what I got to contend with?" Harriet asked Stan.

Stan looked over at Bob who had been holding his arms out in indignation, but was now just looking defeated and rubbing his chin.

"If any of them come sniffin' around here, what am I supposed to say?" Harriet tipped the gun at Stan demanding an answer.

# Back on the Farm, Continued.

"I really don't like telling other people what to do," Stan replied. When Harriet just kept looking at him, he added: "They oftentimes won't do what I say anyway. Or they get it wrong. Or they just ignore me!" Stan's demeanor changed. His voice rose. In another moment though, he had calmed himself. He rolled his hand. "…Or they misunderstand. Or they just don't have the wherewithal to bring it off. Or they're just damned lazy. So mostly, it's just a bother and a real waste of my time."

"You kill people. Isn't that like telling them what to do?" Harriet lifted the gun barrel.

"No. That's like telling them to stop."

Stan took a long pull from his cigarette and then put it out, right there on the table.

Bob was surprised as hell it didn't get him shot right then, especially when he stared up at Harriet while grinding it out. That little wisp of smoke which marked its extinction, Bob fully expected to match Stan's extinction. 'Shit,' *he* was *married* to her, and he wouldn't have tried that.

"If I hadn't just asked you a question and was *expecting* an answer, Mr. Cool-as-a-Cucumber. I would blow that grin right through your face," Harriet growled. "That, plus, I am trying to understand the charm with which you can sway over this dimwitted husband of mine."

"Now Harriet… Ya got the gun. Do you have to provoke people likewise?" Bob protested.

"Shut up! Apparently I do," Harriet barked.

"I'll take it as a good thing." Stan nodded.

"You kin take it anyway you damn want, or sell it," Harriet retorted. "But before I blow you right outta that chair there, I wanna know - just outta curiosity, and maybe for a good laugh - just what your idea about what your further plans here might be?"

"Further plans? " Stan laughed, but watched Harriet's eyes.

"You know, I don't believe I've ever noticed a man studying my eyes so thoughtful before? Perhaps I shoulda started out my female career pointing a gun at more men." Harriet glanced at Bob.

"A sure attention-getter. I'll give you that!" Bob nodded.

"And then you can shut the hell up! again," Harriet repeated. "Now what is it? What are your plans here?"

The hired man, Stan, took his time wiping his mouth with the paper napkin. He took the soiled napkin and gathered up the squashed cigarette and ashes into it, folded the bundle and placed it neatly to the side. He smiled at Harriet. Harriet smiled back. She checked to make sure the safety was off. Stan nodded.

"You know, this idea that you think hard about what you want to become in life, and then study to become it, and then you go out and find a way to make a living doing it, and then you either succeed or fail in the attempt for the most part - isn't really how it works."

Harriet raised her brows. "So how did it work? Let's say, I'm curious."

Stan's brows furrowed. He seemed easily annoyed at being interrupted and his voice rose.

"What more often happens is that you are doing something - which you think is going to make things the way you want them, more or less - when something else happens, something comes along, usually completely out of the blue, and you have to make a choice. And then that choice decides what you're *actually* going to do with your life. And after that, you really haven't a lot of say about it. Excepting maybe, how long you intend to continue."

Harriet nodded. And Bob copied her nod, as he relished his pork chop. Bob was getting lulled by Stan's soft words, and had begun to eat his unfinished meal. Bob reached for the butter knife.

"And don't you move another inch." Harriet swiveled with the gun towards Bob. "And also, shut up!"

Bob jerked his paw back quick as a puppy could. "I didn't say a thing!"

"I am just *reminding* you."

"So what happened to me was," Stan emphasized. He continued in a soft voice. So soft in fact that each of Harriet and Bob had to lean closer to hear. "I had a run in with the *Federal Government*." Stan rolled up his left sleeve and turned his arm palms up to reveal a bar code blended somehow to the underarm skin of his left forearm.

Bob leaned in. And Harriet appeared almost to have forgotten the gun, resting it on the table as she leaned over closer to have a good look, too. And for a time the two of them just looked on the seamless skin patch of Stan's with wonder.

"Why that looks just like something on the side of a package of Wonder Bread," Bob said, poking it. Harriet nodded.

"How much does something like that cost?" Bob asked, with some admiration.

"Shut up!!! Good Lord," Harriet barked, emphasizing this by slamming the gun on the table.

Stan looked at the embedded tattoo of sorts somewhat wistfully with the regard of a old veteran for a platoon logo. Bob moved his lips while mumbling the numbers printed up the side. It registered on Harriet that this was suddenly turning very strange.

"Who *are* you?" Harriet said.

# The Marriage Therapist

"I had what psychiatrists would later come to call, an 'ambivalent' relationship with my mother," Stan continued.

"You know Stan, we ain't asking anyone around here to talk about their mother," Bob interrupted. "But that Federal Government part of it, I believe we both find interesting."

"I believe it's germane to the tale, Bob," Stan explained.

Harriet nodded emphatically. Bob shrugged.

"Who knows how or why, but I can hear her voice just running around in loose in my head… just this utterly uncontrollable bitch! Even now."

"She died?"

Stan nodded, and shook out another funny looking cigarette from the carton.

"How'd she die?"

Stan lit the cigarette with a shaking hand. His head twitched to the either side several times, until inhaling the joint and blowing out slowly visibly calmed him.

"Car accident. House fire. Ice pick through the eyeballs, or decapitated and mangled viciously in a bloody threshing machine accident, which was investigated and cleared me of all blame when I was only 12. What does it matter? The point is, that it stopped the voices!" Stan emphasized.

"Okay. That sounds good," Bob said, cautiously.

Harriet nodded emphatically.

"But then, as I carried on with my life and built a *career*, in … Somalia, Iraq, Afghanistan - any place with fucking *sand*, it sometimes seemed! I heard voices, in the native language… The psychiatrists later said that I must have been a very sensitive boy." Stan interrupted himself. "Not that a female ever makes sense. No offense, Harriet."

"No, Stan," Harriet said. "I can see where you're coming from. I can't say as I've had the easiest time with them myself."

Stan nodded his appreciation. "But these were in a foreign language. And they were always female, very domineering, very demanding, very curt, unloving... and hectoring." Sam waved frantically in the air as if to ward off a flock of attacking crows.

Harriet frowned.

"So I had to bow out and headed back to the States, where at least I could understand the whole jabberfest." Stan sighed and took two more long tokes of his cigarette... 'which Bob was thinking might be 'drugs'?

"You want a toke?" Stan whistled with held breath.

Bob started to nod and say "Yes", until Harriet glanced his way and Bob shook his head and said "No" softly, pulling his hand back.

Stan nodded.

"Oh, they would start out in the morning discrete and humble enough, just say asking what time it was, or asking about this or about that, real pleasantly, or reminding me to do something. Then progressing to asking me what I had planned for the day, and then adding something to that plan of the day, plus a request to help them with one or two things, if I could, before I did any of that which I had planned for the day, and finally beginning to sound hurt and petulant when you tried to beg off in order to just get a little of your own momentum going... Or maybe just start the day with a cup of coffee first before being harassed, from one end of the kitchen to the other, for Christsakes! Making requests and giving orders... And then, of course, they're on you for swearing and cussing and getting upset... at something else! not them, for Chrissakes. Because you're trying to be good about that. And by the way, 'Whereever did you get so sour and suspicious?' and 'How come you have to get so incensed by the slightest little request when I ask it? I don't mind doing things for you?'"

Stan nodded. "Yeah, like you can ever remember anything I ask you to do!"

Neither Harriet nor Bob could gather Stan was addressing.

"I *tried* talking to it. I *tried* being reasonable. But all it would do was to ignore me, or ask why I was upset. Or finally, after I was just about to flip out, "are you *okay*, Stan?" Like it really cared! It would ask, all *concerned* like. Until finally, I decided. I'm going to have to *kill* it. I had been killing a lot of people for Uncle Sam by that time; so it only seemed like the next logical step to begin killing some for myself." Stan glanced around as if looking for support.

"Well now, I can kind of see your point." Bob nodded finally. "I mean, I can kind of see how a man could get to that state." Harriet swung the gun towards him. "Or, you know, begin thinking that way if it was a bad day or something, or you had taken sick. …And then immediately putting it out of his mind, of course."

"You see there are some women," Stan continued, "I don't know why, but they are like powerful broadcasting stations. Their yammering thoughts just stream out! And the closer they get the more powerful they get. Until murder is about the only thing. And then it's a territorial thing, too. You have to defend the boundaries of your psychological territory. Like that poet Frost says, "Good fences make good neighbors." So. In a way , it's like any mission. You get a reading. You triangulate. Then you go in on a Sweep and Clean." Stan made some Delta Force movements.

"This' all fine and good," Harriet said, not really believing all this. "But I don't see why you had to go and get my husband involved in all of this."

Stan exhaled slowly as he sat up. "I thought it would help your marriage."

What?!"

"You see, Harriet!" Bob exclaimed. "I told you Stan was bound to have a real good reason for whatever it was that I was doing!"

"You were *raping* someone!"

Bob shrugged acknowledgement. "Okay."

"That's marijuana you're smoking, isn't it?" Harriet demanded.

"Yeah?"

"That's illegal in this state."

"I… I thought they just passed a law." Stan scrunched his brows, as his train of thought was dislodged.

"They may have just passed a law in this county. But we are still proud citizens of the United States. And it is still very illegal to smoke that in the United States of America." The gun barrel rose up and down as Harriet said the United States of America. Stan's eyes followed the gun barrel as Harriet recited this, and he started laughing, until he started coughing. Putting out the joint, he looked up at Harriet with reddened eyes. "My bad," he said.

Harriet nodded.

"Where was I?"

"You were telling us how you were doing some *Marital Therapy* with Bob here." Harriet poked the gun at Bob. "Out in the dark, in the woods, with some woman called the Muffin Lady, who you drug from her car and raped and assaulted." Harriet nodded.

"Oh, yeah. That's it." Stan rubbed his face.

"For a while, after moving Stateside and mustering out I made a living for myself doing Marital Counseling," Stan continued.

"He did Marital Counseling!" Bob exclaimed to Harriet.

Harriet cocked the gun. "I've got ears don't I?"

"Just sayin'," Bob squeaked. "So maybe we could *both* listen and learn something?" Bob suggested.

"You just ain't got a brain in your head, do you?"

"You got to admit, the blush has kind of gone off of our relationship over the past couple of years, Harriet."

"?" Harriet looked at her husband, speechless.

Stan nodded.

"?" Harriet looked at Stan, speechless - before some harsh words came to mind. "Oh, I'll bet he was just super at that!"

"Many of my patients swore by me," Stan declared.

"And I'll bet the others swore at you." Harriet laughed. "That is, if you hadn't cut their tongues out. Or beat them senseless, and *murdered* and *raped* them."

"We considered every form of therapy. We didn't take anything off the table. You take violence and rape off the table and it's no longer a fair encounter. It's not a natural environment. The men are at an immediate disadvantage. How can you expect to plant and grow the seeds of a lasting relationship, if you deny one of the partners their natural inclinations?"

"You've got to admit, the man makes sense." Bob nodded.

"You see who thinks you make a lot of sense?" Harriet nodded to Stan.

Stan slowly shook his head. "Reality doesn't care what we think of it, Harriet," Stan replied. "In fact, it doesn't even know we exist."

"You mean, what's around us doesn't even know we're here?" Bob slowly glanced around. "You see there Harriet. Now something tells me, *that* makes a lot of sense." Bob's eyes widened with the shock of an epiphany.

Harriet rolled her eyes.

"I was *Impotent*, Harriet. And now I'm *not*!"

"What in the world are you bringing up *now*, Bob?"

"What I've been trying to *tell* you, for the past several weeks, Harriet! But you just keep mumbling, "Go out and milk the cows Bob," and turning over and going back to sleep," Bob implored Harriet. "Like I'm not even there. …That I'm no longer *impotent*."

"Oh, Bob. Would you shut up about *that*!"

"But it's important!"

"*Now* is not the time!"

But he's a *therapist*."

"He's a *serial killer*!"

"Well… Can't a person be both?"

"I swear! I am going to shoot you, so full of holes… that it will spell your name. R.o.b.e.r.t. (.B.o.b.).W.e.e.d.s. right up and down that newly empowered little weenie of yours," Harriet swore.

"Harriet! I'm *potent* again!"

"So can we talk about this *later* then?" Harriet turned with the gun emphatically.

"Sure. Sure. ...Maybe then we could have *little* Bobs?"

Harriet cocked the trigger again.

It was quite a while before anyone spoke. Until finally, Harriet shook her head, as if to wake. "So." Harriet coughed. "*Can* we move on to this... so called, *government* involvement?"

"Your hour is not yet up." Stan smiled.

"Good." Harriet leaned back and threw her bead back on Stan.

"Yeah. How does that barcode thing there on your arm supposed to work?" Bob asked.

Stan looked at Harriet. Harriet nodded.

"Well," Stan replied. "If I get in a sticky wicket somehow... say the authorities have located me and are about to move in, or my mission has been compromised, I simply run this patch on my arm through the scanner of any nearby store and my information is immediately uplinked to a massive central server, an internal clearinghouse of all digitally originating information worldwide, where this code is recognized and activates a very Black Ops insertion and rescue operation. It takes about 24 hours to be fully staged and operational. So it's not a complete failsafe."

"Huh!" Bob grinned, touching it. "What does the store read out on the cash register say?"

"It says, Have a Nice Day! ☺" Stan replied.

Bob laughed. "That's great. That's real nice."

"And it gives you 50 cents off on a frozen package of peas."

"Umm."

"He's joking, you nitwit," Harriet said.

"No I'm not, actually." Stan replied. Bob looked vindicated. "And it's just such comments such as that, which have served in the past to destroy this man's fragile masculinity. To the detriment of you *both*, I might add."

Harriet was abashed. "I don't know. It just come out..."

"It's true. That sort of attitude just comes out, runs out of her like puss." Bob nodded.

"Well. Words *do* hurt. And it's something to think about, especially if you are trying to improve your relationship."

"I'll try to do better."

"Good," Stan said.

"And I'll help all I can with it," Bob made a heartfelt offer.

"Good then!" Stan smiled, clearly enjoying the cathartic moment he'd helped sponsor. He stood. "Let's all join hands then in a short prayer… and then see what's for desert."

"Oh cripes!" Harriet had set the gun on the table and was wiping the sweat from her hands before clutching those of the others. "I got so wrapped up in that article in the Times that I plumb forgot about fixing the dessert."

"It's no matter. It's no matter." Stan nodded.

"Yeah," Bob agreed, holding out his hands.

"Let us pray."

# Benny Green

Benny Green rolled off of his mistress. "I just *love* this recession!" He crowed.

High profit, blue chip businesses were scrambling like rats to deal with their cash flow problems, and Benny was gobbling them up right and left like a hungry alley cat. 'And some *really* high rollers were tossing some *really* nice mistresses out onto the streets', Benny thought, kicking the sheets gleefully.

Benny, himself, had just upgraded to a *natural* blonde, *ten* years younger than his former mistress for near the same outlay… with better teeth and a lot less profanity. He glanced to the left. And she had just *risen* from the bed and was in the kitchen *presently,* steaming his latte and warming his brioche, which she was soon to bring out on a tray with a fresh squeezed glass of orange juice and a freshly printed edition of the mornings news. And this had been going on for *months.* Still, he nearly had to pinch himself to believe his good fortune. 'How the very rich lived!'

Benny was just finding this out now, himself, from *her,* the natural blonde debutante from some rich eastern Ivy League school.

He didn't know which school. And frankly, he couldn't care. It was probably all lies. But, 'damn it if I'm not living like one of the one percent', Benny exulted gleefully in his new found prosperity. He snapped open the front page of his prim morning paper, as his mistress unfolded the legs of the bed tray over his ample midsection.

"Shit!" he exclaimed, following the story down below the fold. "Someone popped the Muffin Lady."

His mistress quietly mopped up the spilled juice.

There it all was, just below the fold: the tale of a gruesome rape, complete with a decapitation - if the sources were to be believed. And there, way down at the bottom, was a hint of federal involvement. Which Benny took to mean right away that he'd better call Delores.

"Delores," he said over his cell. "You may be getting some

visitors soon from *back East.* Make sure those *files* we discussed in the *pasteboard box…*"

"It's too late, Benny. They're already *here.*" Delores' voice shrunk to a whisper. "And I've been trying to hide that *box* as well as I can, but I don't know…"

"So… that's great!" Benny exulted. "That's perfect. That couldn't be better! Now you just sit back and let happen what they have to do. Okay?"

"You sure about this?

"I'm sure about this. That's what I really want." Benny could hardly contain his glee.

Delores acknowledged and hung up. "Well, now,' Benny thought, 'I think we know who the rat is - errr, was.'

There *always* was one. Which was why Benny was *always* prepared. It baffled Benny how so many people felt that if things were going good, then they were always going to go good. Baffled him, but it also made him a lot of money. "Lots of people didn't anticipate the recession and so it just gave me an opportunity to be of help," Benny snickered. And " lots of big wig criminals refuse to acknowledge the risk of getting caught," he wagged his finger at his mistress. "But sooner or later, getting caught is nearly a certainty." His mistress nodded nonexpressively, agreeing with his wisdom; seeing she had lived the fallout of it, firsthand, Benny figured.

The first mistress he'd ever had, had served him warmed up pizza and flat beer on the lid of a limp cardboard pizza carton in a sour bed, all the while finding fault with whatever scheme Benny had been cooking up at the time - until it had invariably descended into a screaming match/ food fight. 'Why am I screaming at my mistress?' Benny had to ask himself at the height of it all. 'This is nuts!' But at the same time, the thought of changing her out just hadn't occurred to him, as all of the other mobsters had complained of the same problems…

"Jeeze, we may get older, but we *do* get wiser." Benny smiled at his blonde bedmate. She smiled back. 'Perfect teeth and such a lovely smile', Benny thought.   And for about two seconds Benny Green was a satisfied man.   Because Benny Green had Satisfaction Deficit Syndrome.

'But with all this new business he anticipated coming in - maybe he could trade up again?  And what would that be?  Maybe a sixteen year old, fourteen, thirteen…?  That could be a little risky.  How young are they supposed to get?  Maybe someone who just *looked* fifteen!  I mean, really naïve.  That sounded about right,' Benny considered.  'I never could get laid for all the rice in China at that age.  And maybe now he could make up for that.  But how would he *find* someone like that?'   Southeast Asia?  But he really wanted a blonde.  Maybe the Ukraine or someplace?'

Benny made another call to Doris.  'Then again…'  He hung up.

'Nope.  Better not pull Doris in on this.'

# Later At Benny Green's Office

Benny glanced over his *Times* at Duane, who was picking his nose, and slapped him with his paper. "Get your finger outta your nose and start doing what I just asked you to start doing."

But Duane just started digging deeper.

"Didn't you hear what I just said?"

"Sure," Duane answered.

"What did I just say?"

"You said… Oh." Duane removed his finger "Sorry. I get lost in …thought, Bennie!" he realized.

"It's understandable," Benny replied. One thought was about the largest log Duane's intellect could step over. Anymore and he just had to go around.

'Duane. What kind of a name was that?' Benny asked himself. 'The kind of name his dead sister, may she rest in peace, would name her kid,' was Benny's answer. He ate. 'He got "lost in thought". And he followed Benny around like a stray dog, always had. But he *was* loyal, and he knew how to keep his mouth *shut*, two very valuable character traits in Benny's line of business. The other thing Duane could do was the heavy lifting. Because Duane was extremely strong and huge and ugly, that is, menacingly so. All of which made Duane a good messenger in Benny's line of work. Benny never needed a delivery receipt. His clients never misplaced his meaning.'

"We have a lot to think about." Benny gave Duane a pat on his huge broad back. Another trait that Benny hadn't thought to think was that Benny could be nice to him; Benny could be considerate, without it looking weak. Everyone needed to love something. It *was* lonely at the top. And Duane never took advantage. Duane wasn't smart enough. Plus, Duane was 'blood'.

Benny glanced over at Duane, who was picking his nose again, and slapped him with his rolled up paper! "Get your finger outta your nose and start doing what I just asked you to start doing. Didn't you hear what I just said?"

"Sure," Duane answered.

"What did I just say?"

"You said... Oh." Duane removed his finger. "Sorry. I got lost in ..thought. Again!" Benny laughed happily. A crumble of snot hung on his index finger.

"It's understandable," Benny replied. "So you got it now?"

"I think so," Duane said. "We're being *in-vest-ti-gated*. Which is a *good thing*."

"*That's right!*" Benny smiled. He re-seated himself and unrolled the front page article he had been reading for the fifth time. "Now we know who the stoolie was."

Benny was been reading about the grisly murder of Nancy Loomis, the "Muffin Queen". It was all there on page one, with much more in the continuing article on pages 7 and 8. How the hell she had gotten herself whacked, Benny didn't know. But what he did know, now, and what was interesting was that the Feds were involved. And since he couldn't see how any state lines might have been crossed in the commission of said crime, there was one likely reason for that being the case... a racketeering charge.

'Oh, that Loomis was a piece of female work,' Benny thought to himself. 'Runs a million dollar business using all those computers and spreadsheets, but she still had to come to *me* when she needed some dough,' Benny congratulated himself. 'Thought I was a moron, too.'

"It's incredible how many people *without* money think that the people *with* money are morons." Benny shook his head. Duane took the cue and shook his head also.

But that was one of the things that gave him an edge in this business. The other was that Benny could *anticipate* things.

Benny looked over the top of the *Times* at Duane, who still hadn't set about doing what it was Benny had asked him to do! Even though he had snapped the newspaper twice! He looked as though he had taken the long route around another thought of his. Benny sighed. "Whenever you engage in criminal activity, there is always going to be a stoolie. It's just the way it is," Benny explained to Duane. "So the thing is to *prepare* for it, which is what we've done now. We have salted our involvement through bogus loans to various, handpicked businesses in the area which I've been trying to get my hands on for years, and now, this is my chance." 'There,' Benny thought. 'I've explained it about as well as it can be explained.'

"That sounds good Bennie!" Duane cheered.

"It is Duane!" Benny smiled. "Because when the Feds - being the bureaucrats they are - are going to go looking for files, because they *like* files, and they love a paper trail. And then, they are going to find *these* files and *my* paper trail. And then, they are going to use *these* files to begin investigating for evidence of 'involvement' of *others*. That would be 'me'. And *then*," Benny smiled, 'they will not *find* any involvement of others. Because all of these paper trails? I made them all up!"

"I like that," Duane said.

"Thank you Duane," Bennie said. He raised his finger. "Which *means*, being the bureaucrats that they are, that they are going to re-double their efforts to find and *uncover this* involvement of others. Because, *being the bureaucrats that they hope to remain*, it would be career suicide to find that there *isn't any involvement* on the part of so-named others after expending the monies and time which they have already expended to find this involvement of others *and* gone before grand juries. All of which - between the investigations and the litigations - is going to be my cue to *begin* my involvement!" Benny cried gleefully and pounded the desk. "Because all of these formerly healthy, profitable, hand-picked companies are going to really *need* my money by then, to defend themselves against all these investigations brought by their government against *their* involvement with me! It is so beautiful, I could just kiss the opportunity! Because I. Just. *Love*. My. Government! Remind me to get a flag. I want to hang it right over there."

"That would be real pretty and patriotic too Benny," Duane said.

"Thank you Duane," Benny said. "Why don't you go over to Pete's now and fetch us a couple of the blue plates, like I asked you to do?" Benny handed Duane the money. "You buy."

"Gee, thanks boss!" Duane smiled, fingering the money, and left.

"Damn! I feel good," Benny exclaimed to himself. And he settled into his desk chair which was pointed at the door while reading the newspaper article through again, while waiting for Agent Curtis and that other one to arrive with the bogus files in hand. 'If he remembered correctly, that other one of the federal agents in this area was a real 'looker'.'

# Back at the Jail

Ruth had run out and rustled up couple chairs so that Leland could now sit four people in his office including himself. They were mismatched. Some were a bit taller. Some were wood, some steel. A couple had padding. Leland figured it all worked out, what with the different people's physiques.

Ramey/Nancy were the hardest to suit. Ramey wanted to remain in his cell. Nancy wanted the best chair and wanted to move it right up front. In fact, Leland had had to kick her out of his own chair several times already. Ruth had tried. But whereas Ramey would listen to Ruth and do as told, this Nancy alter/ego would have none of it. Where she came from she ran things. 'And apparently she didn't feel the Kimmel Sheriff's office was any different,' Ruth thought, glaring at Ramey's backside.

"She just looks ridiculous in pearls," Ruth whispered to Hailey.

Agent Hailey shrugged. Agent Hailey was depressed. Her *partner* had dumped her off here, while presently he was in the big city calling in the reserves to process a bonanza in hot new leads harvested from Benny King's offices. Whenever Hailey called, he told her, "Look, precious. You're doing fine. Just keep following up on any new leads *there*, and I'll keep you in the loop *here* for sure. Gotta go!" 'What leads?' Hailey thought. 'I'm sitting here in an office of losers, transsexuals, and lunatics. And I'm not even sure, where I fit in.'

"I've been cooling my heels here for at least a week now with nothing, as far as I can tell, to show for it except a wardrobe that must have come from the Salvation Army and a kit of dried up cosmetics and mascara. I look like hell. And it seems to me like I'm having to do everything! Where is the evidentiary reply?"

Ramey/Nancy swiveled her head like in the Exorcist, as she spoke.

The real Ramey rubbed his sore neck.

Leland nodded at Hailey.

"Sorry," Hailey replied. "But it seems my *partner* is useless. He said he sent it off. But, when I check, headquarters has not got a record of receipt. Nearest they can figure is that it might have mistakenly been placed in with a shipment of something else, going somewhere else... They suggest we resend whatever else we have and they'll work with that."

"The fucking *Government!*" Ramey/Nancy tossed up her hands.

"I'm afraid I'd have to agree with that assessment Leland," Ramey replied softly.

Leland demured.

"I assure you all," Agent Hailey emphasized rising and stepping to the front to address them all. "That I have *never* seen or heard of something like this happening ever before. In the FBI we are nothing if not fastidious to a fault with evidentiary material. We are backtracking, as I speak. We are re-checking each step of the process. That many samples just can't disappear. We will find them." Hailey emphasized this by lowering a fist and tapping the desk softly.

# Agent Curtis

Agent Curtis could feel the noose tightening, and he loved it. Because of questions related to the nature of the Muffin Lady's death, they'd gotten a search warrant of Benny Green's offices. And while processing the warrant they had discovered - kept in a cardboard box for easy transfer off the premises in the back hallway by the dumbwaiter - a separate, portable collection of files. Payload!

Agent Curtis took what appeared to be one of these files out of a cardboard box on the passenger's side as he hopped out of his Suburban and strode across the street into an older brownstone. The building was in Benny's mother's maiden name and so hadn't been covered under the current warrant. 'This guy has more nests than a rodent. Just a warren of corruption,' Agent Curtis was thinking as he banged on the dingy green metal door just off the second floor landing. 'Who knows where all these doors lead?' He thought, glancing around. 'I do,' he thought, answering his own question. 'A person could tell by the odor...'

"Wadda ya want?" A voice crackled out of the tinny speaker with chipped paint.

"Federal Agent Benny," Agent Curtis said in a clipped voice. A moment passed. "We have a need to talk."

"Funny. I am feeling no need."

"Open up, and you will."

"This wouldn't be Agent Curtis, the alpha dog of Federal Bureau Division 12, would it?"

"How'd you know?"

"It's yur piss ant knock," Benny remarked through the tinny speaker, as the buzzer sounded.

Agent Curtis strode in carrying the file. Evidence was one thing. But confronting the bad guy was another. For one thing, you could gather a lot of information just by observing the suspect and how they reacted when confronted with some damning evidence. And for another, it was just, damn *fun*.

"If you would have just told me it was an old friend, I would have opened up right away." Benny extended his arms.

He sat behind an enormous desk. So enormous that it took up nearly the whole room. Which was probably part of the plan Agent Curtis surmised. By the time anyone could be over or around the thing, Benny would be long gone out the rear door. And where that led was anyone's guess. Plus, the desk itself was of a polished hardwood. Possibly reinforced with a bulletproof steel liner, behind which Benny could duck in case a conversation got out of hand. But what Agent Curtis had in mind was finally going to happen in court.

"All your old friends are dead Benny," Agent Curtis replied curtly. "It's not a good list to be on."

"If you're here about the Muffin Lady, I had nothing to do with that."

"So you say."

"So would *anyone* say, who didn't have anything to do with it. Which would include several million people by last counting within a twenty mile radius," Benny retorted. "You Federal people. You get an idea in your head that someone is a bad guy, and it just seems to stick there. Nothing can dislodge it. No amount of good works…"

"You've told me before how much money you gave to the Sons of Italy."

"That's not my only charitable contribution."

"Save it, Benny. I just stopped by as a courtesy call."

"Oh?"

"Yeah." Agent Curtis waved the file. "I thought I'd give you a chance to do your packing. You're heading for the Big House soon!"

"Ahh! Somewhere in the sun, I hope."

"All of the companies you are purchasing portions of with illicitly gotten funds are right in here. And we're going to have a money-laundering case against you so tight this time, that you'll spurt just like a fattened tick."

"Can I have a look at it?"

Agent Curtis shook his head. "No."

"What'd you bring it for then?" Benny whined.

"For show and tell. Just to see you sweat, Benny."

"I don't think you've got anything in there."

Just then a car alarm sounded. Agent Curtis turned his attention to it. Then Agent Curtis noticed that Benny Green hadn't. Both paused for a moment.

"You think I'd be stupid enough to leave the box of evidence in my personal Suburban?"

Benny looked like he was searching for a good retort to that, but had swallowed it.

"I'll bet there's nothing in that file," Benny reiterated.

"And you'd be right," Agent Curtis showed him the blank sheets of paper.

Benny frowned.

As Agent Curtis was stepping out the door, Benny took out his cellular phone. Agent Curtis turned back. "Oh," he said. Benny quickly hid the phone. Agent Curtis laughed, pointing to where Benny had hidden his phone, and shook his head.

"I forgot what I had to say!" Agent Curtis smiled, waved and left.

After Agent Curtis had surely left, and the door had surely shut, Benny made several calls on his traceable phone to several names at all the companies on his manufactured list. He drug them into a confusing conversation for a time, and then excused himself pleasantly and hung up. If they weren't accessible he left a cryptic message. Then he began to think about dinner and maybe going out with his mistress tonight to see the Lakers perform. Sometimes celebrity fans would attend, and she loved that. And when she was happy, the sex was better. Not professional on her part perhaps, but true.

# The Campaign Café

Stan had finished his Sunday meal and packed up. The evidence of their crimes was by now certainly lost in the catacombs of the Federal Bureaucracy. Nevertheless, even a small town sheriff could look at tire treads and count boot prints. And two guys in a manure splattered pickup was what was looking suspicious in these locales of late. Sooner or later the Sheriff was bound to be stopping by the Weed's dairy farm, and it was better for all concerned if Stan weren't around.

Stan explained to a nodding/crying/head shaking, disheveled Harriet, so that she could later explain it to Bob (over and over) that there was nothing for them to worry about, while she worried herself nearly sick. The physical evidence was long gone, and without witnesses all the authorities had was a body. Which, Stan also added, was probably long gone by now, too.

Bob started blubbering, after he had finally driven Stan into Kimmel and stopped in front of the Campaign Café. "I think me and Harriet are actually going to make it now…" Bob Weeds wiped the tears welled up in his eyes. "Fourteen years now of TV, cow shit, chicken dinners, birthing and bawling, and feeding, and milking… I wished you didn't have to go!" Bob blubbered. "I know we done some bad things, but…" He didn't finish.

"Just remember, if we happen to encounter each other again, we're *strangers*. We can never admit to having met," Stan warned him.

Stan had briefly toyed with killing them both - it would have been cleaner - but for some reason just hadn't 'gotten around to doing it'. Maybe the laid back farm life was getting to him.

"I know. Our lips are sealed by Federal Imprimatur." Bob had remembered the term Stan had fashioned. In fact, whenever he said it, he started to bawl again.

"Got to go," Stan said curtly, turned his back and left.

Bob put the truck into gear and slowly drove away. This chapter of his life was already beginning to fade into memory, though Bob couldn't recognize it at the time. By the time his first two kids were nine and ten it would be like it had happened to a different man. Bob wouldn't even have known himself.

# Cash Under the Counter

Probably another reason Stan hadn't killed Harriet and Bob Weeds was because there was some 'unfinished business' nagging at him. At least that's how it felt. Something about his stay in Kimmel County felt as if he'd left the house and forgotten something. And Stan didn't need all the complications another two killings would bring.

After Bob Weeds had dropped him off, Stan stepped into the Campaign Café for a cup of coffee and a little time to think. He sat down at the counter, where his back was to the street and to the other patrons. Several tables at the far end looked to have collected laptops and phones and coats and briefcases and papers enough to signify an encampment. Judging from the snippets of conversation which drifted Stan's way, this was the press corps domain. They looked the image. Rumpled shirts, loosely knotted ties, coats tossed over the backs of chairs and with eyes staring into laptops. These guys looked as desperate as the story they were chasing. From what Stan could make out, they were trolling for who was writing what, and who had found out what, and how, and where? Stan figured he would've been more of a shoe soles on the street sort of fellow. But what did he know?

Anyway, the place was packed, even in this off hour. Some kid in the corner looked like he was talking to some members of an organized tour. The waitress looked to be running her legs off, so Stan rose to refill his coffee himself.

"I can get that for you," the waitress said, as Stan stepped behind the counter and reached for the coffee pot.

"Uh. Thank you." Stan tipped his head. "You look a little short handed."

"You think?" She smiled. The way she smiled made Stan think that she might either own the place or have an interest in its success. "I don't suppose you cook?" She joked, surveying Stan from top to bottom.

'Was there a *sexual* overtone to that?'

Stan took a look around the café again. Across the street was the Sheriff's office.

"Yeah. In fact, I'm quite good at it." Stan smiled. She wasn't half bad looking, he thought.

"Right. I know. Back yard barbeques. Hot dogs. Hamburgers. And every Sunday morning you make waffles." The waitress smirked, from across the aisle, as she refilled more coffees.

"Nope. Army. Third division Rangers," Stan said.

"Not much interest in K rations here," the waitress replied.

"Not much interest in K rations there," Stan rebutted.

The waitress continued with her other duties. She yelled to the cook in the back several times. And several times the cook in the back yelled back... in a patois of Spanish and English. Stan continued to sip his coffee.

"Are you just making conversation and pulling my chain, or would you really know how to do a short order job?" The waitress asked as she walked back to Stan to re-fill his coffee.

"I'm not gassing you." Stan shook his head. "To tell you the truth, I sort of miss it."

"Ha!" She wiped the counter around. "How badly you miss it? You miss it today?" She tossed her head to indicate their overstressed kitchen behind.

Stan figured for a moment. "I could," he answered.

"Forty dollars to finish out the afternoon. And if it works out, we pay you under the table for a month until we see how everything goes," she said in a low voice.

Stan nodded finally. Then he rose and walked behind the counter. The waitress/owner, who introduced herself to him as Carmella, handed him a newly laundered smock and pointed him towards the kitchen. Stan nodded to the other cook, who looked up without registering any surprise whatsoever. That alone told Stan quite a bit.

"This is your grill. This is your area. And this is your counter. I'll clip the orders here," Carmella said. Stan nodded. Carmella clipped an order there, stared at him, then spun the thing like a roulette wheel. Stan had the ticket on its first pass. He was a quick study.

# Livin' On The Down Low

In Stan's experience, if a fellow wanted to remain as inconspicuous as possible, a guy could do worse than hooking up with a married woman. They took care of all the meddlesome particulars about slinking around and remaining invisible. They were a constant source of information. And what's more, they kept their mouths real shut.

As long as you kept them happy - which wasn't hard, they just wanted to get laid and to have some fun - they'd mind their own business. His 'mysteriousness' was part of the draw. 'Poor schmuck husbands', Stan ruminated, 'aren't exactly the last word in *mysterious*.' He continued to ruminate as past memories rose up.

The Burnetts owned a couple cottages which served as a sort of town motel. Carmella put him up in one. Bed and board and two hundred a week cash under the counter, plus all the sex Stan could manage. Carmella had eaten a few too many hash browns to be bouncing around on top any more, but she was a willing vehicle.

She liked to scream, which at first had Stan alarmed.

"What the fuck!" He stopped mid-stroke. The Sheriff's office was just across the street.

Carmella groaned and laughed. She was slippery and wet and breathing hard. "That chaste Sheriff of ours is probably asking Ruth to close the side window now."

Apparently having Carmella shriek was 'business as usual' around there Stan discovered. Oddly, it seemed to put the whole town in a better mood and on an even keel. As the purveyor of this communal gift, Stan was even given an obliging nod now and then, as he strode about the small town. In the matter of a week or two, Stan was accepted as completely into the fabric of the town as Bob Weeds, with a history spanning generations, had never been.

Something sad about that, but Stan didn't dwell on it. He mostly stared across at the Sheriff's office and tried to figure what it was about that place which had him itchy as a bug on a skillet.

# Peter Barnett

Peter Barnett woke in the high rollers suite of the Lakeside Casino and rubbed his face. His head hurt something awful. He staggered into the shower, dressed carelessly and made his way down to the café for some coffee. Each ring of a payout bell was a little mental whip hoisted in the hand of one of the Devil's own minions. Or that's how it felt, as he passed through the casino on the way to his breakfast.

Everywhere you went in this place, you had to pass through the gambling in order to get there. 'Not by accident!' Peter Barnett was sure. He made the café, only to sit down gingerly and place his order, when he thought to walk back into the casino again and check his standing. (The poached eggs Benovicchi looked interesting, though more than likely a little rough for the come and go hash cooks of his café to master. Nevertheless, this was a kitchen. And the personnel here had mastered it. Or, anyway, he would taste and see if they had.)

These black out spells were driving him crazy. For example, he couldn't remember this morning whether he was up or down. 'He had to stop this drinking while he was gambling. '…Maybe even when he wasn't', he thought, touching his head gingerly.

He shuffled back out to the accounts window to check his stats. And what he saw made his bowels churn and his genitals shrivel. He was *sixty thousand* down! This couldn't be right. He wasn't *that* bad of a gambler, drunk or not. A cold sweat broke out on his forehead.

The pasty guy behind the counter must have seen lots of shell-shocked faces before. Because he didn't register any emotion outside of what could have been a slightly complacent smile. "Bad news?" He asked.

"Only if you hate prison," Peter groaned. "Just kidding!" He quickly amended, managing a sickly smile at the security camera which rolled 24/7.

The pasty guy laughed politely and drifted back into his slightly complacent smile.

'Maybe this will all look better after breakfast,' Peter thought.

He was just biting into his Egg Benovicchi, thinking that fry poaching really gave an egg the kick that it needed if it was going to rise in people's memories above all of the innumerable other breakfast eggs they'd had and that maybe they should give this recipe a tryout at the Campaign Cafe at home - when he got that call from Carmella. "I keep telling you Carmella not to bother me midday when I'm in all these meetings involving city business…" he responded without listening, when Carmella just went right on talking, interrupting *him* for once.

"Well the café needs you *here*," Carmella said. "Between the tourists and the gawkers and the press and our normal crowd, I'm threatening a prolapse trying to keep up with it all. I haven't even had a chance to count the receipts. It's all sitting in a big pile of money in our back office! I need *help*!" Camella barked. "The *city's* doing fine."

'No it's not,' Peter was thinking. He rubbed his forehead. 'This Egg Benovicchi wasn't really all that it was cracked up to be', he finally decided, putting down his fork. He was feeling a little sick.

"Alright. Great. Fine. Just give me a couple days to tie up things, and I'll fly up there in a jiffy."

"A couple of days is not 'a jiffy'."

"Listen. I'm wearing a lot of hats here, and I can't say much more than that. But if you don't want one of those hats to look *very* black, you'd best give me a couple more days."

Carmella didn't know what *that* meant. And it was probably best she didn't. So she let it go. "By the way", she added. "I hired a new guy. Pretty much sight unseen. Says he can cook."

'Sight unseen', was pretty much the way Peter liked it. And if he hadn't *heard* anything, that would have been that much better. "Sounds good," he said. "One day trial. Cash out after the first month unless he pans out?"

"Yeah."

"Okay." Peter nodded. "Look I've got to go. The town council is filing in now. Expect me in a couple days or so."

"Okay." Carmella sighed.

"Love you." Peter disconnected. 'Two days to win back the town's sixty thousand.' He swallowed the remainder of his coffee. 'He'd better get back to work.'

# Nancy Gillis Girl Reporter

Nancy Gillis was only 15 and as her reportorial career was going, the blush was already off the rose. Sure, she could continue writing for the Kimmel High Wolverine. But if she wanted to remain in the Big Leagues she was going to have to use her *access*. Her editor back at the Times had made that as plain as a seasoned editor could, who was trying to delicately negotiate a conversation with a 15 year old girl in a far away state. "You are still in school and learning, " he continually was saying. They had much more experienced, seasoned, savvy reporters who could do the frontal assault thing, he reiterated.

But Nancy Gillis had already tapped every source she knew. Drew, the boy who was running the tour service, gave her a couple things he had filched from the Mercedes. A toothpick, which didn't look to be something the victim might have used. And a slug he'd found fallen under a tire… which she'd already photographed to accompany a first person account of her initial arrival on the crime scene. The Sheriff wasn't speaking. And she didn't trust the other reporters. They were jealous competitors. And Mr. Wallace, their journalism teacher at school, had as much as advised her that she was getting into deeper waters than he wanted to wade. "You're just starting a career here, Nancy. But I'm 5 years from retiring out of this school district. That is, if I can keep from stepping on any toes. The school district just *hates* paying out benefits."

"Now, you want to go on writing sensational stuff that will get picked up by the Times, that's fine. But they're your editors then. You understand? I can't be associated with this stuff. Not that there's anything wrong with it, you understand. But it's very dangerous to play in the Big Leagues, if you're not a Big League player, or at least have a Big League Club behind you. They'll eat you up and piss you out. And I'm not young enough to play stickball with them. They always 'stick it' to the little guy, you see, when things go sideways. You want to go back writing about cookie sales, or Mr. Buckley's class efforts to repopulate the riverbank with natural growth rhododendrons - then I'm right here. Okay?" He shut the door.

Nancy nodded. But she groused silently to herself, 'Gawd! How did men get to be such old ladies?' Fifteen years of age and she was *already* beginning to realize how vigorous, questioning people could drive themselves crazy or get themselves into serious trouble just trying to make something happen! Perhaps she was gleaning a little insight into her own father's situation. 'Life was such a vipers' pit of conflicting passions and cowardice, all trying to circumvent one another'. She hadn't met the serial killer and hoped that she wouldn't - at least until he was well behind bars. But they might very well have seen eye to eye on some things. She was already feeling the urge to kill something.

These difficulties rolled over and over in Nancy's head, as she rode her brother's bike with the card in the spokes around the small town. Finally, having worked up a hunger, she sat down at the counter at the Campaign Café and ordered a burger, shake and fries. Another newbie was working in the kitchen and the clatter in the place was about twice the usual level. 'Well, that made sense,' Nancy figured. 'At least these crimes had brought a little prosperity to my 'depressed rural community.' Nancy practiced phrasing it like a veteran reporter. Then she decided to make a list. "You want to know something? It's people", Mr. Wallace had been fond of saying. "They'll either be able to tell you what's going on, or even if they don't know, you'll find out how much they care. And while something no one cares about may be important, it's not *newsworthy* - unless somehow you can *make* them care. Got that?"

'Okay,' Nancy thought to herself, 'who is there in this community who might know something, or have access to knowing something, who I might be able to cajole into helping me?' She liked the word 'cajole'. She practiced writing it in the margin several times.

By the time she was done she had about 13 names.

One by one, she crossed each and every one off, until, as she saw it, she was down to one or maybe two.  The first was Ruth, Sheriff Leland's secretary.  And the second was that wild card, Agent Hailey.

Then she made another list, remembering another thing which Mr. Buckley had said:  "Put yourself in the interviewees' shoes," he had said.  "What would talking to you, accomplish for *them*?  What carrot can you offer?  What do they care about?"

Nancy Gillis started that list.  She was just about done with it, before she remembered to eat.

She glanced up after gathering together her burger and noticed the new cook looking at her.  She smiled.

He nodded slightly, and gave her a small smile back.

# Pitching Ruth

"How's it going?" Nancy said, after she'd introduced herself.

"How's it going? Is that the sort of cleverly crafted question which keeps a writer publishing just below the fold of the New York Times these days?"

"It's called a 'conversation opener', Ruth," Nancy replied. "And why are you trying to break my balls like this?"

"My name is not 'Ruth'. It's Ms. Haphelstot to you. And where in the world did you get that expression, "busting my balls," Nancy? You're a 15 year old *girl*."

"Sorry. But I've been hanging out at the Café with the other journalists, and that's just how professional reporters *talk* Ruth."

"You *have* no balls."

"It's a euphemism. A turn of phrase."

"I know what a euphemism is, little girl. And I'm been intimately acquainted with a lot of turns of phrases in my day, and they're all just dicks calling themselves Richard, if you can translate my French. And I'm surprised Carmella would put up with it over there. And I have half a mind to call your mother, that is, your father Nancy. And I'm *not* Ruth."

"Sure, you are."

"Not to a 15 year old girl, I'm not."

"Are you going to be a *prude*?"

"Yes! When I am employed in a professional capacity." Ruth was adamant.

"The Sheriff calls you Ruth," Nancy whined.

"That's because he's the Sheriff."

"Well, I'm a *reporter*," Nancy retorted hotly.

"You're a *gossip*," Ruth replied. "And a little, 15 year old one to boot."

"That's not what the New York Times thinks."

"What the hell do you want, Nancy?" Ruth said finally.

"You may call me Ms. Gillis, please."

Ruth sighed.

"Alright. Ms. Gillis it is. What would you like to know, Ms. Gillis? And does your *father* know where you are?" Ms. Haphelstot asked tartly.

"Look. Maybe we got off on the wrong foot here Ms. Haphelstot," Nancy said solicitously. "Because I'm merely calling to see how the investigation is going. We haven't heard much about it out here, where there is so much fear and so little real knowledge! And I bet you can imagine how conjecture will fill in all those vacant spaces! ...!!! So, I thought I'd call and nail down a few *facts*."

"What facts are those?"

"Is it true the Federal Bureau has been dragging its feet in analyzing the evidentiary material in this case?"

"Where'd you get *that* idea?"

"Well, despite the scuttlebutt I overhear at the café, I figured it couldn't be because our Sheriff is at fault. He strikes me as a pretty sharp cookie and a pretty resourceful law enforcement officer to say the least." Nancy hoped she wasn't slathering it on too thick.

"He *is*."

"Well then, what's the hold up?"

"Oh for Pete's sake. I shouldn't be talking about this. But I'll be damned if I'm going to let Leland take the fall here. The *fact* of the matter is, we don't know *where* the evidence is. We sent if off to the FBI, two weeks ago. We got back an initial dribble of information. And now it's like it's fallen into a black hole."

"I'll bet Lelan... *Sherriff* Leland's pretty upset."

"Would you call shouting, upset?" Ruth asked.

"Um." Nancy replied, writing.

"But I can't fault Agent Hailey. She's done all a body can do, as far as that goes. In fact, I think she's very embarrassed. Her organization has really let her down on this one."

"Um huh." Nancy said, taking more notes.

"But at least we still have the bodies."

"The bodies?" Her pencil stopped.

"Yeah. You know, how when people are killed, their bodies often remain."

"Do tell," Nancy replied sweetly. "And where are they?"

"That I can't say."

"But you're sure they are still there?"

"What? Why would the bodies be missing?"

"Well. I don't know. But the other evidence is, right?"

The line went silent. Nancy could almost feel the vibration of Ruth's mental gears turning through the phone; first slowly, and then at hyper speed.

"You know what? Something's come up. And can I talk to you a little later about this, Nancy?"

"It's Ms. Gillis."

"Certainly Ms. Gillis. Just let me handle this bit of new business, and I'll get right back to you. Okay?"

"Sure," Nancy agreed and hung up.

By the time Ruth had locked up the Sheriff's office and headed out in the Sheriff's car, Nancy was following closely, pedaling hard on the far right side of the road… the playing card in the spokes humming. People rarely looked for tails, Nancy figured, riding bikes on the opposing sidewalk.

Nancy lost her after six blocks, 3 dodged dogs, one shopper, another biker, and a small boy going the opposite direction (poorly), but by then Nancy had already figured out the only place Ruth could be headed.

Ruth had reached the butcher's and was talking animatedly and motioning with her arms, by the time Nancy arrived. Nancy saw them head towards the meat lockers together and stood wondering what she should do.

She leaned her bike against the bushes and walked over to the

Sheriff's car. Ruth had left it unlocked. Nancy looked in the back hatch window but saw nothing as there was a security shade drawn. So she opened the clam doors and saw plenty of room for a small girl to hide.

Nancy considered. Today was Friday. So there was a good chance her father wouldn't be back until the wee hours and then not up until eleven or twelve that next day, which gave her lots of time. She still had a bottle of water and half of the hamburger she'd purchase at the restaurant wrapped up in a napkin.

Nancy hopped inside and closed the clam shell doors softly behind herself, just as Ruth was exiting from the butchers at a calmer pace and looking relieved.

# This Jail is Getting Too Small

Sheriff Leland was pacing. Agent Hailey was on the phones. Ruth was making busy in the outer office after informing Leland with great relief, for no reason that Leland could figure that, "The bodies are still there!" And Ramey was crying from the jail: "When am I getting out of here?!"

"It's no use." Agent Hailey hung up.

Sheriff Leland turned.

"No one knows *anything*. For about a week there we were getting good information. And now, I swear, it's as if they have lost all the samples." She looked both dejected and embarrassed. "I'm sorry, Leland. The FBI is usually a *very tightly* run organization. I guess you just have to believe me about that. But I just have no idea where all our evidence is, or who has it, or why we don't know. Trust me, this isn't how it usually works."

Leland shook his head and rubbed his temples. "It's not your fault," he said.

"I *know* that," Agent Hailey replied.

Leland looked at her, tossed up his hands. "Fine. So where does this put us?"

"Ruth?" Leland called. "Could you go back there and ferret around a little through all of those empty evidence lockers and see what we might have left, if anything, from that serial killer crime scene investigation."

"Sure!" Ruth called from right beside him. She was glad to be escaping the vicinity.

"Sorry I snapped at you there, Leland," Agent Hailey said.

"You're the least of my worries," Leland laughed.

Agent Hailey huffed.

"I'm sorry!" Leland swore. "I just meant that you're not my *problem*."

When Ruth returned, it was with a small baggie in hand. "I found this one thing," she said. "I would suppose the plastic seal got caught in a crack so that the baggie didn't empty into the shipping box."

Sheriff Leland held it up against the fluorescents and looked it over. "It looks like manure. A small piece that fell from a boot tread, is my guess."

"I think that's a good one. Seeing as we're surrounded here by dairy farmers." Ruth chuckled slightly.

Leland frowned. "Well, maybe we can glean a little more out of this one than what first meets the eye."

"Let me go! What about my patients?" Ramey called from the back cell.

"Trust me, you're patients are not gonna want their dental work performed by a practicing transvestite," Ruth shouted back at him.

"They might! If they are in enough pain…"

Leland tucked the baggie in his jacket pocket and hooked his head for Agent Hailey. "You wanna come?"

"No. I think I'll just sit here and sulk like a little girl. Then maybe shoot myself with my revolver."

Leland just didn't seem able to win today.

But when he strode out of the office, Agent Hailey smiled and followed.

# Merlin's Clinic

"Are you going to talk, or are we going to ride like this all the way to the Vet's?" Agent Hailey asked.

"I'm just trying to stay out of trouble for a few minutes, so I can concentrate on matters at hand," Leland answered, staring ahead down the main street of town as he drove.

"Goodness, you sulk like a little girl," Agent Hailey said.

Leland stopped the patrol car.

"Why are you trying to bust my balls here?" He asked. "I didn't lose the evidentiary material. And I didn't blame you about it."

"Oh, here we go: "ball buster", "loser". ...any other moniker you want to add?"

Leland nodded. "You're fingering your weapon."

"Oh." Agent Hailey blushed, drawing her hand away. "Habit."

"Uh huh," Leland said.

They drove the rest of the way to the Vet Clinic in more silence - not knowing that all the while, Nancy Gillis, girl reporter, was hidden under the back security shield taking note of everything.

When they arrived, Merlin was dealing with a scared housecat.

"Best stay out for a minute!" He called from beyond the door.

They heard a low, rumbling yeaorrrwwwl!. Then it was like all hell broke loose inside the closed room. A jar broke. Finally it was all quiet again.

"There," Merlin said appearing. He shut the door behind himself. Merlin's brows rose. "What have you brought me?"

Leland held out the sample.

"I meant 'her'," Merlin smiled, most courteously. Like Leland, he was another of the single, marriageable men in this small community. And a new, good-looking woman was like a greased pig dropped ring center at the local rodeo. Men became offish fools in an effort to grapple them quickest. Merlin removed his long leather gloves.

"This is Agent Hailey." Leland introduced her reluctantly. "And you needn't kiss her hand."

"How do you do?" Merlin gave Agent Hailey his most winning smile. "You can call me 'Bones'. He reached to shake hands.

"I'm fine, thanks." Agent Hailey shook. "I believe Sheriff Kelly here has some evidentiary material he thinks you might be able to help us to better define."

Leland laughed to himself at Merlin's quick reassessment.

Merlin turned away to do so, facing up to Leland. "So! It's back to the Private Sector again?" He smiled.

"I need you to look at this and tell us what you can. I think it's probably cow manure fallen from a boot tread."

Merlin looked at it. He opened the bag to sniff. He spit on his thumb and index fingers and reached in and made a quick slurry of it to sniff. "It's pig shit," he said handing it back and smiling again at Agent Hailey.

"Can you tell us any more?" Leland asked.

"Possibly," Merlin said cryptically. "So where are all the other boxes of evidentiary material you retrieved from the scene? The government gets all of *that*, and *this* is what I get?"

Agent Hailey was about to open her mouth when Leland spoke. "That's right."

"You give the government their hair and tissue samples, their tire treads, boot tread casts, their spent bullet casings and blood and slugs along with God-Knows-What-Else-including-possible-belly-button-lint-off-of-the-rapist I'd-suppose... what that you scoured the area for and found and must have delivered to them in umpteen cardboard evidentiary boxes all nicely sealed in plastic and labeled 'such and such' - and *me*, you handle a little pellet of pig shit?" Melvin asked.

"Yeah, that's pretty much the all of it," Leland responded.

"Do you realize Leland, for even one millisecond, the disrespect with which you employ the Private Sector?"

Leland stared at Melvin blankly. So did Agent Hailey.

"Well, there it is." Melvin shrugged and spread his arms haplessly. "Nothing to be done about the *Bureaucratic Mind*, ... the old *forms in triplicate* lockstep, I suppose. Except to add that I would guess that the entire resources of the Federal Government brought to bear on your problem have *not* been able to provide you with the information which you *suspect* might come from one little cubelette of pig shit handed to the correct person in the Private Sector. Am I right then, in assuming this?"

"There you go." Leland and Agent Hailey both nodded.

"Which! I will take as a concealed compliment and proceed to do my examination."

"Okay." Both Agent Hailey and Sheriff Leland nodded.

Merlin took the sample into his small lab, mixed a measured amount of it with various reagents, heated it for a specific time, and then placed the concoction into a small laboratory spectrometer which gave him a number which Merlin wrote down on a small scrap of paper. Then Leland and Agent Hailey followed Merlin into his office where he sat before his computer.

"Depending upon what the farmers around here feed their pigs, the pigs excrete more or less nitrogen and phosphorus. Pigs and other domesticated animals around here subtract from the total carrying capacity of the surrounding ecosystem by helping to bury us in all their shit..." Merlin droned on as he trolled the computer screen.

Nancy meanwhile had slipped out of the patrol car and was overhearing as much as was possible with her ear pressed to the clinics thin window panes, thankful that Merlin worked with all of the blinds closed. She took notes, writing phonetically any of the words she was unacquainted with for further clarification later. While Merlin continued...

"...the most toxic elements of which are phosphorus and

nitrogen. So! The Bureau of Ecology runs a contest in which each pig farmer submits a shit sample to see who of them is feeding their animals diets which produce the least phosphorus and nitrogen waste in their shit. Which isn't really as easy as it sounds. Every pig is a little different. So the farmer has to really know their animals. The Bureau gives them informational brochures to get them started, and then the farmers take it from there. The winning farmer gets 500 Eco Credits which can be spent on all sorts of things such as clearing away a swath of forest which has been hindering him, or draining a damp portion of the pasture or shoring up a creek bank. And if you go on their website you can see how the various farms around here stack up - who is in the running and who isn't. So, let's do that."

Merlin brought up the website on his computer. And there was quite a long list of farms. Merlin looked at the number in his hand and went down the list. "Well, our boot does not work at one of the better farms. It looks like he falls in somewhere right around here…" Merlin selected out three farms with competing pigs.

Looking closer, Merlin remarked, "Hmmmm. This is interesting. Bob Weeds is in here. Usually, he doesn't play. Says it's because he doesn't want to have anything to do with the government. Which is understandable." Merlin glanced at Leland. "Except that he seems to have changed his mind. And he's doing pretty well. Each of these past three months his farm has risen in the stats, which is unusual. Usually it's only the competitive ones near the top which continue to improve and grab the credits."

"Why do you think Bob would be doing better?" Leland asked.

"Knowing Bob, I would say it's because someone has been giving him help." Merlin nodded.

"I think maybe we ought to see who that someone might be," Leland said. "What do you think, Agent Hailey?"

"I think that's a good idea, Sheriff Leland," Agent Hailey replied.

Leland and Merlin made a little more small talk, and then Leland and Agent Hailey left. This gave Nancy Gillis just enough time to run back to the Sheriff's SUV and jump back in the clamshell, shutting it softly behind her.

# Gunfight at the Weed's Corral

The Sheriff's SUV spit some gravel as he backed it up and turned it onto the main road. After passing through town, it felt to Nancy as if they were going at a pretty good clip on their way out to the Weed's farm. No one spoke and all Nancy felt was the jostle of the road, and all she heard was the whine of the tires and the whoosh of the passing air. Nancy wrote this down.

Finally, Nancy felt the crunch of the tires on the roadside gravel as Sheriff Leland brought the SUV to a stop. "That's the Weeds farm up ahead. That cut-off to the left leads to it."

Agent Hailey nodded.

"I figure we ought to have some sort of a plan worked out before we go in. There's Bob, his wife Harriet, his dog Vomit - who is one, big, mangy son-of-a-gun of a Great Dane, though there is absolutely nothing 'great' about him. And then, there may be a hired man, who would more than likely be our lead killer, if things are as I suspect them to be. Or two hired men. Who knows?"

Agent Hailey nodded.

"So. Since they know me, it's probably best I drive in, in my Sheriff's vehicle well announced. This should draw everyone towards me, including the dog, fleas and all. Our killer, or killers, may think this is a good time to slink away. So I'd suggest I drop you off half of the way in, and you perform a flanking maneuver in order to cut off our main perp if necessary, and also to provide me back up if necessary - and vice versa."

"Works for me," Agent Hailey replied.

Leland nodded. "Fire a shot if you need help."

"Got it. Gunshots mean the ball's in play." She smiled.

Leland shook his head. 'It's that *attitude*,' he thought.

Nancy licked her pencil and wrote all this down.

Both Leland and Agent Hailey re-checked their weapons before starting out. Nancy Gillis could hear them clearing the clips and working the cylinder action before placing the weapons back in their holsters. Leland drove back onto the blacktop and up the road about a quarter mile before turning off to the left up a rutted road. He stopped after several minutes. Nancy heard Agent Hailey leave the vehicle and shut the passenger door softly. Then the SUV moved ahead.

Nancy could tell when he arrived at the farm, which was on a knoll, by the sound of the vehicle dropping down into the low gear and the sound of the dog barking. "Hi ya Bob." Nancy heard the Sheriff shout. She wondered why he didn't get out. Then she heard the sounds of the dog barking, growling, scratching the doors and slobbering on the windows. "Hey Bob! Oh Key-rist!" Nancy heard Sheriff Leland cuss as he started the car up again. "I'm going to have to drive this damn car right up into their living room in order to have a decent conversation," he muttered as the car lurched forward, the dog growling and barking and chewing on the tires as the SUV ground in low gear up the knoll.

"That would be a good place, right there, to park your car Sheriff," Bob Weeds shouted.

Sheriff Leland yelled to him through his front car window. "You want to shut this damn dog up in that shed there or something Bob, so's we can talk?"

"What is it you wants to talk about, Sheriff?!"

"Oh, I'm thinking it would be Sheriff's business Bob!" Leland shouted from out the crack in his driver's side window. The dog growled and chomped at Leland's nose. "You want to curb that damned dog of yours?!" Leland ordered.

"I don't think he trusts you Sheriff." Bob laughed.

"Would a bullet make him more cordial?"

"C'mon Vomit!" Bob ordered. The big dog cocked his left ear. "C'mon!" He ran into the shed before Bob, and Bob shut the door after him. Leland opened the door and stepped out of the car.

When Bob reappeared he was carrying a rifle.

"There's no need for that Bob," Leland said. "At least yet. I just came here to talk."

"You brought yours."

Leland heard a screen door slam and from the other side of the road came Harriet, and carrying a rifle also.

Leland sighed. "Good afternoon Harriet." He waved.

Harriet cocked her head but didn't say anything.

"Well I can see that I'm not going to be invited in for tea and cakes! So I'll just get right to the point."

"That would be a good idea," Harriet called out, walking closer.

"You know the last time I was here you two weren't coming out to meet me with guns," Leland observed.

"That would be when you was working for the farmers around here and not someone else," Harriet observed.

"When was the last time you cum out here?" Bob asked. "Cause I can't even remember Leland."

Leland looked at Harriet. And he didn't like what he saw. She was usually the more neighborly of the two. Now, she was staring at him like he'd never grown up in these parts. "What do you mean, "I'm working for someone else," Harriet?"

"I mean, back when you represented us as Sheriff. I'm havin a hard time now believin' I voted for you. Who are you working for now Leland?"

"I'm still the Sheriff of Kimmel County Harriet. Here's my badge and there's my car."

"Things aren't quite like they seem anymore, we been findin'." Harriet raised her gun.

"Harriet, I gotta say. I don't know what in the hell you are talking about," Leland replied. "You want to just put that gun down so we can talk. And, by the way, maybe tell Bob there to put the safety back on his."

"No Leland, I'm not gonna do that."

"You haven't noticed Sheriff that there been some strange things going on around here of late?" Bob Weeds said.

"Yeah, Bob. I *have* noticed that. Two woman found dead with their heads cut off and one of them raped. Now I have real reservations about Harriet being involved in any of that. But I'd thought that I might come out here and talk to *you*. And I have to say, your having a gun right now doesn't make it look too good."

"I've had a gun since I was six," Bob replied.

"That would be before puberty," Harriet observed.

"Yeah? Do you usually carry it when you come out to greet your neighbors?" Leland asked.

Bob spit. "Sometimes," Bob replied. "My land. My rules."

"Well then, I'll come right to the point. Did you rape and murder a woman just south of here several weeks ago?"

"Why do you want to know?" Bob spit. "What business is it of yours?"

"Bob! I'm the Kimmel County Sheriff. When people around here get raped and murdered it's my business."

"Okay."

"And this is how you investigate?" Harriet spoke up. "You drive out somewhere in the country and just ask people if they'd done it? Are you some kinda idiot?"

"Harriet. It just seemed polite to ask first."

"Before what?"

"Before I take Bob here in for questioning."

"Bob ain't goin' nowhere for 'questioning'." Harriet looked real sure of this as she raised her gun towards Leland.

"Harriet. I've got to say, I'm kinda confused about this. Because if your husband Bob did actually go and rape and murder the woman in question here, and then cut her head off - I'd think you at least want to hear about a little bit of the evidence first?"

"Well then, I'd guess that makes him look a little more innocent, wouldn't you think?" Harriet countered.

"Well, to tell you the truth Harriet, I have found, at least with criminals, that wives are not always the best judge of their true character."

"You think I would be harboring a rapist, and I wouldn't know it?"

"Well. That's what I would think Harriet. But now I'm having some second thoughts. I could understand Bob here wanting to hold a gun on me. But why in the world you are taking this course of action has got me puzzled, I have to say."

"If'n you take Bob here down to that jail there and talk with him more'n 5 minutes… intelligent a man as we all know my husband to be, he's also real sensitive and apt to admit to just about anything in order to quell an argument. Isn't that right Bob?"

"You have understood my true nature Harriet."

"He could quell an argument right now by putting down that gun of his."

"It ain't an argument till I pull the trigger. Right now, it's just a discussion," Bob observed. "And this gun is what keeps it on those terms."

"That was well put, Bob." Harriet smiled.

"Thank you, dear." Bob looked a bit embarrassed, grinning back at her.


Leland didn't know what to make of it. "What the hell? You two been to marital counseling or something?"

"How would you know about that?" Bob turned suddenly grim, thinking that perhaps the Sheriff had learned something about his impotence, also. "Who you been speakin' with?"

"It was just a question Bob. Calm down." Leland put his hands out - partly because he was getting the feeling of having walked into some kind of weird parallel Universe where a known couple of marital bickerers were grinning lovey-dovey at each other while pointing rifles at *him*. It could make a fellow's thought processes dizzy. And just then Agent Hailey chose to step out.

"I checked all the outbuildings and looked over the nearby area. Nobody else is around."

Harriet swung her gun towards Agent Hailey, who had her revolver aimed at Bob.

"Hold your fire everybody," Leland spoke as calmly as was possible with his arms held wide as possible. "And we can sort this out."

Meanwhile, Nancy Gillis - who had slipped out the back clamshell door of the Sheriff's SUV in order to better hear and to take notes - decided to snap a photo. Using the war correspondent's slogan: "up at 5 to shoot at 8", she set the aperture at 8 and set the camera shooting mode at rapid. Then she poked her head out from under the front bumper to quickly focus the scene.

When she drew her head back, she saw it was a good picture - if you didn't mind silhouettes. She swore. The sun was behind her subjects. If she wanted to get shots full of facial expression and texture, she was going to have to move about twenty yards to the left and about ten yards closer. There was no way of doing that without being seen. 'But', she figured hopefully, 'they'll be so busy with their guns aimed at one another, I should be fine.' So she gulped some air, positioned her toes like at a track meet, and took off at a run pressing the shutter release and clicking photos all the while. She was so scared she dribbled urine. But it turned out fine. At least the photos did.

The others didn't fare as well.

Harriet saw Nancy spring from behind the Sheriff's front right fender and reactively swung her rifle towards what was initially just a figure in her peripheral vision.

Agent Hailey saw Harriet aiming her rifle at a child and immediately shot.

Harriet dropped, from a bullet through the center of her temple, like a sack of wheat.

Bob looked befuddled for a moment, then started to scream: "You shot my wife. You shot Harriet, you somabitches!" And turned his gun on Leland, who, dove behind a cultivator, left unattached of its tractor there off the drive.

"You are dead!  I am killin' you!!"  Bob yelled and shot repeatedly, the bullets zinging from the frame and blades.  All the while, Leland was yelling: "Stop shooting!  Bob!  Quit shooting that damn gun, would you please?"

"No Leland, I'm not gonna do that," Bob said, as he calmed down some for a better aim.

Leland had his pistol in hand, prepared to fire.

But there was another "pop!", and Bob Weeds dropped, just like his wife Harriet, to ooze a gathering pool of blood out of his head onto the dry ground.

Agent Hailey strode up quickly to kick the rifles from both Bob and Harriet Weeds hands and then test the couple for signs of life.

Meanwhile Leland strove to extricate himself from under the implement.  "Are you okay?"  He hollered to Nancy Gillis.

But Nancy Gillis, fairly shell-shocked, only nodded, mutely.

# The Dental Beat

Nancy Gillis was just in emotional overload. First she had been scared to death. Then she had witnessed firsthand the two killings.

People arrived. They discussed events with the Sheriff and Agent Hailey. A perimeter ribbon was stretched around the scene. Photos were taken. Evidence was packaged. Bodies were examined and then carted off in Vern Smith's portable slaughterhouse. Nancy's dad was called but couldn't be found. For quite a while, it was as if she were floating above herself witnessing it all from a soundless stage.

Back at the jail, meals were ordered from the Campaign Café across the street. Nancy ordered another burger, though she didn't have much urge to eat. But if she made herself speak up a bit, then she found the adults left her alone. So she ordered her preference and answered their questions. She described what she had done and how she had come to be where she was.

"Chasing the story." Sheriff Leland shook his head. "You are one resolute little woman, I'll say that," he grumbled. "I'll also say... No, I won't. I won't say anything more that I might find myself ashamed of saying later. But... damn!" He turned away from Nancy vexed. "I'll tell you what," he said turning back. "Why don't we put you in here in the cell with Ramey, while we're waiting for your dad to show, so's you don't get into any more trouble. At least over the next hour or so. How would that be?"

"Fine," Nancy replied softly and contritely.

"Okay. Good," Sheriff Leland replied and ushered her off with a wave of his hand towards Ruth.

Nancy followed Ruth into the back cell. Which she found was also holding Dr. Ramey Evans, their town dentist. Although 'holding' wasn't quite the word, as the cell door was left unlocked as any room in a house. She looked at Dr. Evans again. At least she thought it was him. Though it could as well be some dangerous maniac or just a simple lunatic as he was dressed in woman's clothes and wearing make-up. Nancy sat thinking. She glanced at Dr. Ramey again. Finally, she screwed up her courage enough to beg the answer. "Doctor Ramey? That's you, right?" She leaned forward to better peer past his rouge and eyeliner.

"Yeah," Ramey said. He looked pretty dejected, like the Cowardly Lion or something. "Who did you think I was?"

"Well... nobody else," Nancy lied.

"It's not like it looks or what you might think," Ramey sighed. "I just wear this," he nodded his head to the side, "to keep *'her'* happy."

Nancy wondered who Dr. Ramey was speaking of.

But Nancy nodded. Then she went through her notes, filled in a few things, and asked Ramey what a few of the words she'd overheard meant. Then it struck her that there was another story here. After all, the town's dentist disappears for several weeks and then he's found cooped up in the Sheriff's jail? *That's news! isn't it?*

Her classmate Cynthia Baker had had a toothache and had to be driven all the way to Toone's Corners to get it fixed. Missed a whole day of school. She told Dr. Ramey that.

"I'm sorry," he said.

And then she knew a lot of people were upset about their dentist dodging out on them, also. After all, to get to another dentist required driving a long way out of their way. Around town the feeling was that it was very 'unprofessional' of dentist Ramey to just disappear.

"I couldn't agree more." He stared at her with his palms open.

But it hadn't seemed as though there was much anybody could do about it. Even Ramey, it now appeared.

"Right now I'm not in very much control of my life." He nodded.

Both he and Nancy looked around the jail.

'Here Dr. Ramey was, hidden out in the County Jail - for reasons she wasn't aware of - and no one, outside of the Sheriff, knew.' She felt the giddy mania of another imagined scoop rising up.

"Is it a crime to dress up as someone of the opposite sex?" She asked.

"Not that I know of," Ramey replied. "But here I am." Ramey pointed a long lavender fingernail out towards where Sheriff Leland paced. "You might ask *him*."

"Maybe not now, though."

# "So, Where Are We Now?"

"So how many times do you *usually* let a perp shoot at you before you return fire, Leland?" Agent Hailey screeched. "What did you think you were doing out there?"

"I was trying to salvage the situation. One of our leads was just shot. And then, there was a good chance the other one was going to get himself killed too." He returned the look at Agent Hailey. "…right about that!"

"So I'm the bad guy here?"

"No."

"After just saving your ass?"

"I'm not saying that."

"Then what in the world were you out to prove?" Agent Hailey looked seriously concerned. "The guys got a rifle and he's taking pot shots at you… and you're still trying to talk him down?"

"He was overwrought. We had just killed his wife. Bob Weeds probably couldn't have hit an elephant at that range. And besides, I was hiding behind that… that…"

"Cultivator!" Nancy called from the cell area, checking her notes.

They both looked into the holding pen and frowned. Nancy was diligently taking notes.

"Yeah." Leland sighed. "Behind that… cultivator, thing."

Nobody spoke for a while. Finally Leland reached into a drawer on his desk. "Do you ever drink on the job?"

"Only when necessary," Agent Hailey responded, holding out her hand.

Leland looked up under his brows at Ruth as his hand remained in the drawer.

Ruth nodded.

Leland nodded at Ruth, and she brought 3 plastic water glasses.

"Three?" Leland queried.

Ruth nodded emphatically. "Yes. I believe three are necessary."

So Leland poured them all a stiff one, then raised his glass.

"...to the full *extent* of the law," Leland proposed.

"...and beyond." Ruth added.

The three of them drank.

Leland wished he could've had just one shot at what he felt to be the *real* perp. And he wished he knew exactly *who* that was.

Ruth was looking cross-eyed at Nancy, trying to get a rise.

Leland filled them again.

After a while, they were all relaxed, depressed and rehashing the events. Leland had his boots up on the desk. Ruth's spectacles kept falling off her nose, and she was making a bar trick of pushing them back on with her tongue. And after finally accomplishing that, she tossed her arms out and took a bow. Agent Hailey had unhitched the top buttons of her shirt and had her head tossed back cackling at Ruth's clowning.

Leland removed all the bullets from his gun and was sighting through the cylinders. He could see portions of the legs and shirts and shoes of the pedestrians walking past outside his window through the slats in the blinds. "So where the Hell are we now?" He asked the room in general. "What do we now have to go on?"

"Well," Ruth opined. And when she lowered he head to talk, her glasses fell off again, which interrupted her opinion, as she scrabbled around the floor for them.

"You got..." Agent Hailey drunkenly waggled her finger. "Correction! *We* got.... shit." She nodded several times.

"And... *shit* has got us pretty far." Leland nodded. "That Merlin's a pretty sharp character..."

Nancy, meanwhile, had finished her interview and had fallen asleep, leaned up against Dr. Ramey who had his arm placed protectively around her.

Leland glanced around. "Well," he said. "Ain't this a happy little jail?"

# Stan Cleans the Kitchen

'Once you start killing people, it gets real hard to take orders from civilians,' was something Stan had noticed regarding the changes wrought in himself by his life's path. He was having a smoke outside on the back stoop of the restaurant. He was staring out across the back lot to where his small rental cottage stood, wondering how long it would be before the sex with Carmella got stale, and whether that would be before or after her husband returned, when someone strode up on his left stomping on his shadow.

"Why aren't you in there working?"

Patterson was a fairly short man built like a fireplug, with a natural inclination to boss. He strutted about like a rooster with his butt out and his chest up. The guy was a natural irritant. He had a tattoo on his left arm of a sparkplug, with flashes of yellow to indicate electricity like in a cartoon. Stan liked that. But it was about the only thing about Patterson that he liked.

"'cause I want to be here," Stan replied.

Patterson appraised Stan. "What a slacker. You'd best get back in there, if you know what's good for you."

Stan completely disregarded the man.

"You hear me?!" Patterson yelled, leaning in, so that his face wasn't more than four inches from Stan's.

A bit of spittle struck Stan's forehead above his left brow.

Stan daubed at it. He examined his finger.

Then he grabbed Patterson's face in a pincher grip: thumb in the nose and forefinger in the eye, rousting him. And when Patterson tossed out his arms, Stan wrung one, flipping Patterson on his back like a kitten. Then Stan tromped on the man's ribs hard, just once.

'Nothing like broken ribs to take the fight out of someone real fast, and for some time,' Stan mused, staring blankly. Stan flicked open his knife, really wanting to cut into something, while Patterson's eyes grew big as saucers.

Patterson pleaded.

Stan closed his eyes, took a deep breath... put his knife back.

Stan left Patterson groaning in the yard and walked back inside, wondering why he was so on edge of late. He was getting sex.

He considered that maybe it was an existential thing, as he took up his position as fry cook and began riffling through the orders. He was feeling a loss of purpose probably - a loss of mission. Some motivator he'd had, was receding from him, withdrawing like a tide - with still this vague irritant, this mental itch, remaining. This not knowing what was going on; it was a little like the 'fog of war', maybe. Or not.

'Once military, always military', he thought to himself ruefully, cracking an egg.

# Back to the Farm

Carmella was beside herself. The Café was jammed. Outside, a line was snaking down the sidewalk. And she had been running her sneakers off since five that morning. She had added five new waiters and three new cooks in the past few weeks. But they were new and had needed direction. Thank God she had happened on Stan. She had full confidence he'd have the kitchen running like a well-oiled machine given another week or so. He just took over. Nobody complained. So "it was all good", as her husband Pete would say.

Carmella supposed so. She would have loved to know how Stan managed what he had managed, but whatever. It was the one bright spot in her increasingly frantic life. 'Actually,' *two* bright spots.' She momentarily enjoyed where her thighs rubbed.

"Gotta make hay while the sun shines! Right Sheriff?" Carmella chirped to a bleary Leland that next morning.

"Shut up, Carmella," Sheriff Leland said, not his usual polite self and massaging his aching head.

Carmella rested her hip against the booth side as she refilled the Sheriff's cup and murmured in confidence. "I'm sorry Sheriff. I don't know what's gotten into me. I'm just kind of manic, what with all the activity of late, and my mouth bubbles off. You know, we all, I mean the whole town appreciates the lengths you're going to, to apprehend these killers. It's just that the Weeds getting killed has got the whole valley on edge. Not that they were the most popular farmers around. But they had been here for many generations. So it's kind of got everyone shook. Me included, I suppose."

"I appreciate that Carmella." Sheriff Leland nodded, smoothing his head in various spots. "I truly do." He stirred his coffee.

"Okay then." Carmella tapped on the table. "Coffee's on the house."

Leland nodded. Then after Carmella left, he sighed.

'That's what I do,' Leland scolded himself, 'I sigh. This town elects a Sheriff. Murders occur. And what does he do? He sighs.'

Leland berated himself.

Leland thought for a moment, shook his head, and then pulled out his cell phone.

"Merlin?" He said.

"Yeah?"

"I've got work for you."

Merlin didn't respond.

"Pick you up in 10 minutes?"

There was a long pause.

"Sure," Merlin replied.

# Merlin and Leland and his Euthanized Dog

Merlin was already in town, so he dropped by Leland's office and they walked out to the Sheriff's SUV.

"Mind if I drive?" Merlin asked, hopping into the driver's seat.

Leland paused, finally taking the passenger's seat. "I'm just the Sheriff. And this is the Sheriff of Kimmel County's car. Why would I mind?" He frowned.

Merlin didn't reply. Instead, he started the vehicle and headed north.

"North?" Leland asked.

"That's where the bodies were," Merlin answered.

Leland rolled his eyes.

Merlin said, "No?"

Leland shook his head again, and indicated Merlin should keep driving.

"Okay. Where are we headed then?" Merlin asked after they had pulled out of town . It was midday and the sun was high overhead. Merlin turned on the air conditioner.

Leland never replied; his thoughts being on just what it is he might be missing. Harriet had said, "Who are you working for, Leland?" Which was a puzzle Leland had no answer for. Why would Harriet think he was working for someone? Or that he was other than he appeared to be? He'd known Harriet since she was the lonely little fat girl sitting in the room's corner all through elementary school drawing pink and blue tractors which plowed orange and purple rows. He was guessing she owned maybe three dresses in all her whole life.

All Leland really knew about her in the thirty more years that passed were that: she was a lot shrewder than she looked, and that she never took bullshit from anyone. Plus, she was a damned good shot with a rifle. It wasn't like Harriet to believe random aspersions. If Harriet hadn't been 'down to earth' then no one was. So...

Merlin pulled the car over with a quick swerve and stopped.

Leland grabbed the door jam.

'...why would Harriet say such a thing?' Leland wondered again, feeling a painful guilt for no reason whatsoever.

"Okay Leland. I'm tired of this." Merlin fixed him with a look.

Leland was shaken out of his reverie. He paused to reconoiter as the clouds of dust dissipated around them.

"Are we breaking up?" He smiled.

"And by the way, shut the fuck up," Merlin said.

Leland nodded.

"I'm going to say some things, and I want you to listen."

Leland raised his brows.

But it seemed Merlin was having a problem putting what he wanted to say into words. Finally he spoke: "Okay. Here it is. I didn't kill your dog. I 'put him down'. There's a difference."

"?"

Merlin raised his hands quickly. "Let me finish."

"I know how attached you were to Pearly May. It showed all over you. Everyone knew it. But she was riddled with cancer and in extreme pain and there was no denying it. And euthanasia was the best thing we could do - YOU could do - given the circumstances. And I don't *blame* you for it." Merlin paused. "So don't blame *me*."

Leland was astonished. "I never blamed you for killing my ... dog."

"Oh yes you do! You don't *know* you do. But you *do*, nevertheless."

Leland didn't know how a man could respond to this.

"Don't think I haven't seen it before. It's one of the commonest ways a veterinarian loses his clients that there is around. An animal lover loves his animal. But the animal is suffering. So the animal lover comes to the vet and he asks, "What can we do?"

Leland thought about Pearly Mae, which was interesting, as he hadn't thought about Pearly Mae in some time. God he missed her. Especially, what with all of the craziness of late.

"Well," Merlin turned towards Leland. "The answer is, there isn't much we *can* do. We're not God. We don't have those powers. So we give them the choices. I gave you the choice."

"She was a *great* dog," Leland interrupted. "Just the very antithesis of all the craziness that has been going on around here of late."

"And then we may even tell them what we would recommend. But the owner makes the final choice. And then, we put them down."

"That's what she was, Merlin. That's what Pearly Mae was. She was *sane*!" Leland realized.

"What?"

"I can feel it so clearly now, after what's just gone on around here. What with all the awful, vulgar killings, and the shootings of the Weeds. Pearly Mae was *absolutely* sane. And you just can't say that much I'd guess for the rest of us." And inexplicably Leland could feel himself begin to bawl... great racking sobs. "She was so sane. So very sane. She was just a *great, sane* dog!"

"Maybe I'm just crying for the loss of my sanity," Leland said later, with a strangled laugh.

Twenty minutes later, Leland indicated to Merlin that he was ready to roll. And Merlin started the vehicle and pulled out, heading north.

In another half hour things seemed in the vehicle as if they were back to normal. Maybe even better than normal, Merlin thought, glancing over at Leland and then looking ahead.

"You know," Leland said. "It's strange. For the past few months I've felt as if I'd somehow gotten a chicken bone lodged in my throat. But I couldn't figure out where, or when. And now, it's gone." He swallowed a couple times. "Yeah, it's gone."

"So you feel better?"

"Yeah. I do."

"Good." Merlin smiled.

Merlin nodded at a road sign and Leland nodded back. They were almost there. The Weed's turn off was just up ahead on the left.

# The Kimmel County Tour of Very, Very Violent Crimes

When Merle and Leland arrived at the Weed's place, Bobby Spencer's *Kimmel County Tour of Very, Very Violent Crimes* bus - the sign for which covered one side of the old motor coach in bright red cursive letters - was just finishing up its highlight attraction, "Lunch at the Shoot Out!", featuring "Chicken and Biscuits just as Harriet Weeds Fixed 'em". The tourists were wiping the crumbs from their faces with paper napkins and commenting upon a posthumous Harriet Weed farmhand lunch spread, while their kids were running around poking the cows and pigs with sticks.

"You want to waltz in? There's bound to be something left - potato salad, a drumstick or a thigh?" Merlin nodded.

Leland indicated that they'd best park in the shade behind some trees until the tour had run its course. So they watched Bobby as he spoke a little to the crowd, before the tourists in their hats and plastic bags of collectibles rose up from their picnic benches and filed in a fairly neat line through the front door for a tour of the farmhouse. Bobby was wearing the official tour cap and t shirt, as were all of the other school chums Bobby had hired to put out the meal and then gather up the leftovers and clear the tables. It appeared to Leland that Bobby had hired old Jerry Gillis to drive the bus. He had a greasy grey pony tail, a few days growth of stubble and wore a dirty cap advertising Skoal. Leland had a good idea it was that girl reporter, his daughter Nancy Gillis, who had talked Bobby into that hire. Leland hoped Jerry was sober. 'The Gillis girl must be trying to raise the whole family herself', Leland conjectured.

When the crowd was fully inside of the farmhouse, four figures walked out of the barn and began taking their positions around the yard.

In a while, the tourists exited the farmhouse holding up their hands and squinting into the sun. Bobby Spencer switched to a loudspeaker and had quickly run around to head up the crowd and direct their movement. The crowd saw the four figures carrying guns

130

and stopped, clustering where they were.

Then Bobby began his spiel. The other actors represented Bob, Harriet, Agent Hailey and himself. They were all dressed to resemble. Leland figured Bobby must have recruited them from the drama club. Someone had even written them out lines. As Bobby stepped back, the little drama began.

When another actor, playing Nancy Gillis, broke from the crowd and ran forward snapping pictures, Leland reddened. And when the guns fired blanks, Leland's breathing grew ragged and he broke into a sweat.

"You alright?" Merlin asked.

"Yeah. I'm fine," Leland said. But he didn't look so.

With two of them dead, Bobby Spencer turned dramatically and recreated events leading up to the confrontation. He noted where each character stood, the weapon they had, the angle of the sun at the time of the shootout - even the number of bullets expended. He punctuated this monologue by showing them a couple dark crusty puddles which he said still stained the "thirsty soil".

From what Leland remembered, all of that had been destroyed following the investigation, but whatever. Now there were splatters of something, marked off by yellow crime tape, which the tourists touched reverentially and snapped photos of.

It was five or ten more minutes before Bobby Spencer had finished up his talk and herded the crowd of tourists back onto the tour bus. Then, after a count of heads, the tour bus lumbered away.

Merlin was about to drive forward, when Leland stayed his arm.

He nodded at where the actors and waiters were now gathering their things and boarding a small van. After a while the small van lumbered away. They sat for a while longer after that, while Leland collected himself. Then Leland nodded. And Merlin drove the vehicle up into the yard where they parked.

Several minutes passed. Then Merlin said, "You wanna get

out?"

Leland nodded and stepped out into the bright sunlight.

After standing some, taking in the scene, Merlin naturally gravitated towards the barn and the animals, while Leland strode towards the house.

# There's Gold in That There Pen!

Leland sat at the dinner table of the old farmhouse and wondered just what had occurred there. He couldn't imagine Bob Weeds cooking anything worth eating, so it was certainly Harriet who cooked and kept the household. He looked into the dishwasher. But it had already been stacked and run following the tourist's lunch. The whole crime scene was so polluted by now that nothing uncovered could be used to indict anybody now, including a ham sandwich.

'Didn't matter.' Leland was just here to get a feel of the place, to get a feel if he could for Harriet's mental state. He looked around. He couldn't say, in any way, that it looked like the house of a crazy person. It was all fairly clean and orderly. Just about the housekeeping you'd expect a working dairy farmer's wife to be able to manage. There was a magazine about cows and one about guns. Another one over by the plant on a stand was full of household hints and recipes. 'Jeeze,' Leland thought. 'How does it go from *this*, to getting shot?'

He walked outside, squinted up into the sun and noticed Merlin waving to him. So he strode over there.

"I was talking to Mr. Porter here…" Merlin nodded.

"Call me Bill."

"…Bill. And he showed me something."

Bill Porter held up something shining brightly between his thumb and forefinger. "There's gold in that there hog pen!" He said.

Leland looked at it. Bill Porter handed it over.

"Old Bob must have lost a cap at sometime. I was just over here taking care of the animals 'till some arrangements have been made for them, when I noticed this little nugget glowing up at me. Can you beat that? Must have been for doing a good deed," Bill said, smiling.

"Must have been." Leland returned his smile.

"Are you wondering what I'm wondering?" Merlin asked.

Leland nodded. "Bill," he said, "would you mind waiting around here for a while with us? I'd like to make a phone call."

"Sure Sheriff. No problem."

Leland stepped a few paces to the side and called the office on his cell.

Meanwhile, Merlin chatted with Bill Porter about what and all, and about the pigs.

"Ruth," Leland said. "Could you give me Ramey, please?"

"Sure Leland," Ruth said. "What's up?"

"Don't know. Maybe something."

"Okay. Let's hope it is. Here's Ramey."

But it wasn't Ramey who came on the phone.


"Sheriff Leland! I've been in this cell for over three weeks now, or more. I'm starting to lose track of the days. And it seems I don't know one more thing about why I was murdered than I did the night of the attack. What in the world are you *doing* out there?"

"Nancy. Would you please channel Ramey for me? I need some information."

"For your information, I don't 'channel' anyone. I'm just *stuck* here, inside of a *dentist* for Godsakes - and I don't know why."

"I don't know either, Nancy. Now could you please give me Ramey. Poke him, or prod him, or mumbo jumbo him up out of the ether, however you two have it worked out, but give me Ramey please, so that I can get back to the crime scene and do my job. Please?"

Merlin, meanwhile, heard the argument and stepped over. "Who's 'Nancy'?" He asked.

Leland covered the phone and exhaled. "You wouldn't believe... ...I'll have to introduce you!" He smiled at Merlin. Merlin's brows rose.

"Yes? Who is it?" This was Ramey's voice.

"Ramey? Is that you?" Leland asked.

"Yes."

"How do you and... that woman in your head, have things

worked out? It seems every time I want to talk to you, I have to go through her."

"Well. Err, it's difficult to explain Leland. But I think it might have something to do either with, well, just her *nature*, or the way she was raised… I can't really tell."

"Never mind then. Listen. You did Bob Weed's dental work. Did he have any gold caps?"

"Ha! That would be the day. He was a 'fly to Tijuana and have them all pulled kind of a guy.' He joked that he would "spare no expense". He thought that was funny. I think it was his wife, Harriet, who'd thought of the retort."

"Okay, I'd believe that. How *about* Harriet?"

"Harriet? Well, she had pretty good teeth. Not many fillings as I recall. But they were all amalgam. She wasn't the type to go spending money on pretties."

"Thanks Ramey." Leland clicked off.

"That's not Bob or Harriet's gold cap," Leland said.

"Then whose is it, Sheriff?" Bill Porter, who had come walking over, asked.

"That's a good question Bill," Leland said.

Merlin nodded thoughtfully.

# Screening Pig Shit for Clues

Merlin and Leland unhinged the screen door, while Bill Porter pulled out the lengthy cow stall sprayer hose. Bill said that he wouldn't mind in the least helping with a murder investigation. Moreover, that he'd never ever participated in one and thought he might enjoy it. So they had Bill drive the pigs out of the pens. Then Bill shoveled the pens and heaved the muck onto the screens. Merlin sprayed the mud away as a slurry. And Leland scoured the bits of twigs and rocks and other debris left on the screens for evidence.

"It would be pretty nice if whoever died here were our killer," Merlin spoke above the rush of the spraying water he was zig-zagging about the screens.

"Nice. But I wouldn't get our hopes up," Leland answered. "It doesn't figure. If our killer talked her husband Bob into accompanying him on his latest murder/rape - I could see her killing our killer and maybe even Bob, but when I spoke with them, right before both of them getting shot, they were cooing like two love birds. And also, why would she ask me who I was working for?"

"Okay. Let's say it was someone else she killed and had Bob dump the bodies in here. Why would she want to do that? Who in the world would Harriet want to kill? Other than the killer?

"You mean, besides Bob?"

"I thought you said they were cooing like love birds."

"Yeah, but just recently."

Merlin thought about this. "Okay," he surmised. "Then who is a person you or Harriet - or anyone, really - are most likely to want to kill?"

"Someone who's trying to kill me!" Leland laughed. Because this is the way it almost always was in the law enforcement business.

Merlin and Leland stared at each other.

"Someone was out to kill either her or Bob, or maybe just Bob - or maybe our *killer, when they encountered* Harriet and Bob - and Harriet *or* our killer when *he was encountered* - drilled 'em?" Merlin said, just barely making it to the end of that long line of logic.

"Maybe so…" Leland said, as he collected a few items of interest off of the washing screen. "Hey! Hold it up there a moment will you Bill? And Merlin?" He held the items in his palm and mulled them over. "Here, it looks like we have a pretty well gnawed on hunk of a black rubber heel." Leland held it up. Two cobbler's nails stuck out of it.

"Man, those pigs were hungry." Merlin whistled.

"It was a few days before I realized maybe somebody ought to come over here and look after the stock, since nobody was," Bill apologized.

"And here. Oh, this is interesting," Leland continued. "It looks like a portion of a license or a legal identification of some kind. No writing. But it's got that plasticized holographic twinkle to it when I hold it up to the light."

Leland was getting excited. "Okay. It looks like we're going to be out here for some time. I want to sluice all of the mud in all of these three pens and go through it carefully before sundown. Are you two okay with this?"

"Just let me make a few calls," Merlin said, setting the hose and stepping away.

Bill Porter nodded soberly.

Merlin halted and turned.

"Wait a minute," Merlin said. "Holographic ID. And Harriet says, "Who are you working for, Leland?"

"Yeah," Leland agreed. "We may be looking here at the (fecal) remains of some kind of government official."

"Or Operative?" Merlin grinned.

Leland frowned.

"Or several?" Bill Porter's eyes grew wide, taking in the wide expanse of pens.

"It can't be ruled out."

"What kind of government official goes missing and nobody

knows a thing?" Merlin asked.

Leland considered this. "The *worst* kind, maybe." Leland said. All of a sudden, everything was moving very fast... "You two might want to be very careful who you talk to, and how much you say about this for the next while," he added. "Just to be safe," he said calmly.

Merlin exhaled slowly between the crack in his two front teeth.

Bill Porter looked nervous like a man who was suddenly in over his head, or having qualms anyway.

# Influence Peddling

Benny Green got a call from his friend Lazlo in Vegas. Lazlo was also a loan shark and money launderer, but at times they traded leads.

"I got this guy here, thought you might find interesting."

"Oh yeah? How so?" Benny asked.

"Well, he's deeply in debt," Lazlo continued.

"That's a start," Benny agreed.

"He's lost somebody else's money. And if that somebody else doesn't get their money back, he's gonna be in deep shit."

"So he's already in deep shit," Benny replied.

"Yeah."

"And this wouldn't be your money, would it?" Benny asked.

"Well, it could be," was Lazlo's reply.

"Aaahhhh." Benny nodded. This sounded like a two way split. Which Benny liked better than a favor. A two way split was precise and people kept their eye on the play. A 'favor' was a sloppy business and involved a lot of conversation and socializing and most of the time came back to bite you. "And what's his pitch?" Benny asked. "What's his *collateral*?" Benny laughed.

"Well, it's something you might be able to use, but I can't, really." Lazlo let the last words filter out his lips with the smoke from his cigar. "But if you could, then *we* could. But if you can't, then we can't."

"Hmmmmmmm." Benny nodded. It so happens that they were both, at this time, puffing on big cigars - the same brand actually - and letting the smoke filter out from between their lips.

Lazlo belched and waved someone over. Benny, on his end, did the same thing. Benny snapped his fingers and asked his mistress to hand him a ham on rye. Down in Vegas, Lazlo snapped his fingers at a former showgirl and demanded a Chivas on the rocks.

"So why would I be able to use this 'thing' we're talking about, when you can't - or won't?" Benny asked. There was a lot of chit

139

chat and shoptalk embedded in a deal. And Lazlo employed and enjoyed it as much as Benny. And when they were enjoying themselves, they often felt the urge to eat.

"It's a matter of lowkwhoshawn…" Lazlo murmured around an ice cube.

"THwhaut?" Benny chewed, spit out a wheat kernel, and checked his filling. 'What the hell does this woman buy for bread?' Benny had to ask himself.

Lazlo moved the ice cube out of his way with his tongue, then took a sip of Chivas. "It's a matter of loc-a-tion," he enunciated.

"Uh," Benny replied, reaching in his pocket for a toothpick.

"What he wants to *sell* me is a town. …maybe a county."

"A town? What have I got to do with a *town*?" Benny replied. "What am I gonna do with a *county*?"

But Lazlo was silent, letting the matter crawl around the crevices of Benny's lizard brain for a moment, while Lazlo studied a sandwich which was also offered him. He lifted it. Finally, Lazlo decided where he was going to bite and answered. "It's the *town*'s money he lost. He's the mayor, the treasurer, the coroner, the post office supervisor, and a dozen other things as near as I can tell, of the great metropolis of Kimmel, up in your neck of the woods." Lazlo bit.

"And so he wants to trade you the *town,* in lieu of his gambling debt?"

"He wants to trade me his *influence*," Lazlo corrected, chewing. "He figures hi mhight whant tho estahblish," Lazlo took a gulp of Chivas, feeling the ice tap his teeth, "gambling, and maybe a little loan-sharking and prostitution up in his neck of the woods. And he thinks me and him can make that happen. Of course, if I decide not to 'help' him out, then more than likely he goes on the lam, or gets popped, and there goes his influence. So. It's a perishable commodity," Lazlo summarized.

"Aren't we all," Benny sympathized. "How long does he have?"

"Well, there's the payroll he's got to meet, which includes the county Sheriff's salary."

This made Benny's brows rise. "I don't know," Benny said finally. "Currently I'm invested into businesses - *legit* businesses, some of them even hi tech, you'd be proud of me, I am *embracing* technology - and making clean money. Towns *cost* money. They got potholes to fix, cops to fix, and all that shit.. I don't know. I don't see any *money*, unless I go majorly illegal. You know, corrupt with a big 'C'. And then, I still have to put even more money in, you know, to build up the proper infrastructure, to support something that would make it worth my while, considering the risk."

"Benny! I can't believe I'm hearing this. Corruption *always* pays better than legit. That's why we do it," Lazlo swore.

"Aaiiii!" Benny swore. "But I'm getting so tired of talking to that FBI. And the legal fees eat me alive."

"Okay. Okay. Only two words I'm going to say," Lazlo replied. "Las Vegas."

"That's one."

"No, it's two. Look it up."

"I have."

"No. Apparently you haven't, because there's 'Las', and then there's 'Vegas'. Two words."

"'Las' is not a word."

"Yes it is."

"No it's not. What does 'Las' mean? It doesn't mean *anything*."

"It must in Spanish. Or they wouldn't use it all by itself, would they?" Lazlo countered.

"Who knows what the goddamned Mexicans do," Benny replied. "Even if it does mean something, it probably means 'the', or 'before' or 'on top of'."

"'On top of?"

"...or something. And what does 'the' mean? Huh? 'The' doesn't mean anything. It's like a nothing - a, an, empty thought space."

Lazlo sighed. "Okay, look. We're getting off topic here. Why don't we save this linguistic pissing contest for another time?"

"Fine with me."

"Because what I am saying in a language we both know and can *communicate* in is that what we may be looking at here is an opportunity ripe for development. And it might be worth the investment because we reduce the risk, like Las Vegas. They own the desert, and they make the law. No FBI. No lawyers. No courts. No nothing. Just out of state marks. Lots of grain fed marks flown in…"

"I heard you say "*we*"."

"That's right. We split 50/50."

"So what do I do? And what do you do?"

"Okay. So this is it." Lazlo lowered his voice - just from habit, and not because he was afraid of being overheard. It was just habitual to lower your voice when you got to the meat of any conversation. Everybody knew this.

"The guy's short $240,000. It was $160,000, but he tried to gamble his way free. This ought to give you some measure of the guy's ability to self-examine and to self-correct in the face of adversity and of his character flaws."

"Yeah. I got it," Benny said. "Mayor or not, he's just another normal putz with abnormal ambition and what he thought were testicles."

"Yeah. So this is how it is: I give him $120,000. This is enough to save his ass for the time being, but not enough for him to lose that sense of urgency, which is so important for a good relationship to flower. You pay me $60,000, and you're in for half. After that we own him. And you run him and the operation up there, while I raise the money and assemble the backers down here. And we go big league. We put Kimmel County on the map. What do you say?"

Benny thought for a while. "I knew a broad who lived out near there," he said. "One of my clients. Seemed to like it."

"Well there you go," Lazlo agreed.

"Until she got whacked. Some crazy batshit serial killer or some such. Cut her head off. Like, sawed it, with a small knife. Can you believe that?"

"There's a lot of sickos in this world," Lazlo sympathized.

"Maybe. On the other hand, she was pretty abrasive," Benny offered.

"Well, okay. Then there's that. You know, like sometimes a person's karma can catch up to them."

"Yeah, and saw their head off!" Benny laughed. He considered. "Okay, cut me in. And I'll get the money to you by the end of this week. It'll be cash, and I'll have my nephew drive it down personal. Cause you know him and he knows you."

"That'll work, " Lazlo said.

"Okay. Nice bein' in business with you again Lazlo," Benny said.

"The feeling's mutual."

They both hung up, grabbed their drinks and cigars, and sat there thinking.

# Long Distance Call

Peter Barnett rang up Carmella with some trepidation but with his game-voice on. "Carmella!"

"Where the hell are you?" Carmella replied. She was just then placing a platter of biscuits and gravy on a customer's table and slammed it down so hard that the biscuits hopped. Which made the customers' heads hop, which... (Okay. You had to be there.)

"Same place, honey. Sorry it took so long. I got caught in a tight spot and couldn't call. But all is right as rain now. And I'm bringing home the bacon."

"Sorry!" Then, a more hushed Carmella said to the customers, "I'm talking to the mayor."

Her customers nodded. They were tourists, who wouldn't know the mayor of Kimmel from the mayor of San Francisco or that he was Carmella's husband. But they knew the appellate 'mayor' and so were impressed.

"I don't know if I worry more when you sound stressed or when you sound relieved Peter," Carmella said, scurrying out to find a spot of privacy. "I just know that after 10 years of living with you, your high spirits don't put me at ease," she hissed from behind the coats on the back coat rack. "What has happened?"

"Just that my trip down here - though it has had its ups and its downs - has turned out a huge success! I'm bringing back industry and jobs to our little corner of the woods, dear. Kimmel's mayor has come through! You can start spreading the word."

"¡Oh, no, no. Mi pequeña comadreja de un marido," (No way, you little weasel.), Carmella hissed. "I am going to keep it well under my hat until I hear the all of it, and I have you back here under my thumb where your story can be properly vetted and sources checked and corroborated."

"For goodness sakes, Carmella. You want a video of the event? Maybe photos?"

"It would just be more photos of lizards. What are you selling

144

me?  And what have you been doing for *two* weeks?"

"I told you Carmella.  I've been handling some *very* tough negotiations.  But, handling them well, I'll add, now that we're through the worst of it."

"The *worst of it*?  What else *is* there?"

"Nothing we can't handle," Peter assured her.

"*We?*"

"But why don't we talk about the best of it, first?"

"I'm listening."

"I've arranged with a syndicate of backers to finance the development of a huge recreational area right there in Kimmel.  We're talking a construction budget in the millions.  Do you realize what this will do for our small community?"

"A 'recreational area'?  You mean like horse rides and hiking and river rafting and camping and such?"

"Well, more like gambling and adult entertainment… and such."

"Gambling and adult entertainment, in Kimmel?"

"Or just outside!  We'll have to go over the possible locations."

"What's the *bad* news?"

"They gave me $120,000.  But we need $120,000 more."

"$120,000.  They *gave* you $120,000?"

"It's earnest money.  Kind of like a 'commission', you know?  It's my job to help marshal this whole thing through the governmental process, get all the proper licenses and certifications and zoning allotments and such.  I'll be earning my money."

"So why do you need $120,000 more?"

"Because I figured that is what it would take."

"You figure doing all this is going to require $240,000?"

"Yes."

"And how did you arrive at that number?  Right now the office of Mayor pays you around $5,000/year.  How come *all of a sudden* someone from Las Vegas wants to pay you $240,000?"

Peter had no quick answer for that.

"It seems to me that there are all sorts of little nowhere towns with little nominal nowhere mayors who could be had for a lot less than $240,000 - conflict of interest or not," Carmella observed dryly.

"I resent your characterization, Carmella," Peter replied.

"Well, I'm not trying to butter you up Peter. So answer my question. Why, in the world, do these people want to pay you $240,000?"

"Well, it's because they don't actually have to *pay* me any of it."

"Oh, and why's that?"

"Well. It's because I already owe it, to them."

"What?! Peter, where in the world have you gotten $240,000 to *owe* anyone?" Carmella was starting to feel a splitting headache coming on.

"Well, there's where it's been taking me the two weeks to get this all arranged. And why I didn't want to call, before it was all secured."

"Yessssssss? I'm listening," Carmella said, and wishing she weren't.

"Okay. This is how it went down. But it was a good thing! Eventually, this is going to be a good thing."

"Peter, do you realize that we are about three minutes into this conversation and I feel like I am just now getting to whatever it is has happened that you are going to finally tell me? And do you realize that this is how most every conversation we ever have is? Because I have to keep digging and digging and questioning and questioning until I can finally get to what the heart of whatever it is you have to say actually is!"

Peter had been holding the phone away from his ear, so he hadn't heard much of this. But he felt he'd gotten the gist of it, enough to reply with a little hurt in his voice. "Carmella, when you get going like this, it's no help to anyone. Now just shut up and listen for a while."

When Carmella didn't reply, and Peter heard no 'click' of a disconnection, he continued. "What happened is this. After all those meetings with our sister city officials I needed some time off, so I figured I'd just drive into Las Vegas and just look around. All that glitter and stuff, you know. You can literally see the place glowing in the distance."

"You drove into Las Vegas," Carmella sighed.

"Honey, lots of people do it everyday."

"Yeah, but they don't have a drinking problem and a gambling habit."

"It was just for a look around!"

"Okay. So you drove in, looked around, and came back."

"Well, no." Peter sighed.

"God damn it, Peter! How much did you lose?" Carmella felt she might crush the phone. She massaged her forehead.

"Well, only $160,000 at first."

"Only $160,000! Peter *where* did you get that kind of money? You didn't sell our restaurant did you? I don't see how you could have done that without my knowing."

"No. No! Nothing like that. I would *never* do that, honey. I just borrowed some of the city's money."

"You stole money from the town?!"

"I borrowed, borrowed!"

"Then pay it back, back! Right now!"

"I am. I have! At least half of it, anyway."

"Wait a minute. You lost $160,000, but you owe $240,000. What's with the other $80,000?" Carmella kept rubbing her forehead, but more vigorously.

"Well, here's the thing. I figured I'd lost the $160,000 because I'd made the mistake of gambling while I was drinking. I mean, who could lose that much sober? I went down to breakfast the next day and couldn't even *remember* the night before. I mean, I had to walk to the window to check my winnings *before* finding out."

"Peter. How could you start drinking? Again? And in Las Vegas, of all places?"

"I know. I know. Not smart."

"Not smart? Honey, what you have done is so far from 'smart', why, I can't even figure out where it is. You asshole!"

"Look, Carmella. There's no need to take that harsh tone with me. Drinking is a *disease*. Why, if I were dying of smallpox or something, would you be standing there calling me an "asshole"?" Peter replied, feeling hurt and a little self-righteous. "No! You'd be calling a doctor."

"No, Peter. I think I'd watch you die and be enjoying every minute of it." Carmella hissed from behind the coats, seeing the Sheriff suddenly walk in.

Silence.

"I know you don't mean that Carmella. So I'm just going to continue as if nothing had been said, as if you hadn't shared that." Peter sighed.

More silence.

"So, I figured," Peter struck back, upbeat. "That sober, I could easily win it all back. So, I went back at it with a vengeance. I mean, I really worked hard, using all of the skills I've acquired, and playing it tight, playing it right. But. Lady Luck just wasn't with me. And you know, when Lady Luck frowns, well, there's nothing you can do. So I ended up $240,000 down."

"Why $240,000?" Carmella wondered, fatalistically.

"That's when the town ran out of money." Peter shook his head.

"Oh," Carmella replied, wrung out.

"But it's a good thing! Carmella. Because this is where I was able to turn things around, you see, because without that debt hanging over my head, I would never have been able to entice these savvy, shrewd business people down here into investing in our small town way out in the middle of nowhere. But as it worked out, it's as if I played them. Which, I guess I have! They are going to plunge millions into our little town, because they figure it costs them nothing! And all it took on our parts was to lose $240,000. Which, I might add, we plan to pay all back!"

Carmella didn't know what to say. She was dead tired from working in the restaurant 24/7, from listening to the crazy fantasies of a crazy husband and now what could be impending incarceration for embezzlement - plus, just to add another dollop of bad luck to it, possible involvement with shady gambling figures, probably mob-connected. She blinked suddenly as if she'd seen a brief snapshot of her future and saw a shallow unmarked dirt hole somewhere deep in the brushy, bramble ridden woods off a logging road and her buried in a waitress smock or something. Maybe she'd go serve the Sheriff some free coffee. Yes. That's what she'd do. She hung up.

"Leadership isn't always easy, and it isn't always carried out along the direct path," Peter was touting himself into the dead phone. "But the victory is there to be had, and the achievement to be realized for the ones who have the cajones to reach for the ring and stay the course through those tough times of adversity, Carmella. And let me tell you, I'm appreciative of your loyalty. And someday, you'll be able to take *that* to the bank."

# Ralph Bunch Paints 6x10 Foot Chipmunk Portrait

Ralph Bunch has never killed anyone. And he probably never will. And it's doubtful anyone would ever want to kill Ralph. So what's his play? Why shine our spot on him?

Well, life is fleeting (especially around Kimmel County of late) and art is forever. So while life in Kimmel County wound on, Ralph Bunch kept painting his paintings, writing his poems and drinking his alcohol - all in a small hillside studio where he lived just outside of town looking down on the twinkling lights of Kimmel.

Ralph wouldn't say things were going especially well. But things rarely go especially well for painters and poets, and Ralph was "totally prepared for that" - bragging to his wife, who was pregnant with child, as much, just before she left him.

But that was water under the bridge. The years had passed. You suffer for your art, and Ralph's paintings sold well enough now to keep him at just about 15% body fat. So Ralph was fairly satisfied, kind of like a fluffy chunk of green moss is happy enough.

At his monthly art showing/poetry readings held in the bar in the back of the Campaign Café, his paintings often sold from three to four hundred a pop. Ralph used an entertainer's wiles, often pitching the exhibited paintings by reading a poem somewhat reminiscent of Robert Frost.

The paintings and poems often were of someone - or of something dear to someone - living there in the valley. Which meant their wives and friends and relations would attend the fete. And then the person's mother or father or closest would purchase the painting. On other occasions Ralph unveiled a commissioned piece.

The criticism of those who did not like the paintings often fell on the 'painted while drunk' side. While those who did like the paintings often felt that they expressed their own outlook a bit, with the lot of them drinking and getting a lot more vocal as the evening progressed. This was how cultural life was conducted in Kimmel.

Ralph's cultural get-together was considered one of Kimmel's more serious and proper monthly occasions, often covered in the society column of the County Journal. And it ranked just slightly below the Church Social as a place where a person could bring a person of 'serious' romantic interest.

Currently, Sheriff Leland was figuring just how he might invite Agent Hailey to attend with him, without it appearing too much to be what it was or would be, which was a *date*.

*Anyway*, recently Ralph was working on a large painting of George Everlee's prize Guernsey. He was squinting at the thing, while stepping back, trying his best to recover his original inspiration, and under a little time pressure to do so as the 'opening' was only two days away. Suddenly his meditation was disrupted by movement in the blurry background where there, set on the mossy rock of the windowsill was a chipmunk looking back at Ralph with an intensity Ralph had never felt in the face of any animal before. Ralph blinked. The chipmunk blinked.

Ralph stepped further backwards while squinting at his work, then the chipmunk. Then he found himself going through his cupboards looking for crackers and nuts and knocking things aside and chewing off container tops. Later, he couldn't recall what had come over him.

To be honest, the rest of the afternoon was a loss, with Ralph finding himself that evening surrounded by empty cracker cartons, paint tubes, broken brushes, snack bags and empty assorted nut cans, while on the easel in place of his nearly finished portrait of George Everlee's prize Guernsey was a still wet 6 x 10 foot portrait of a chipmunk - more or less. It was probably the most *intense* thing Ralph had ever painted and probably supported the most *paint* Ralph had ever used.. Paint also covered Ralph's hands and elbows. In the mirror his complexion looked as though he were wearing war paint. Ralph Bunch gazed around, still disoriented as if recovering from a very vivid dream, under the bare bathroom light bulb as a dribble of sweat fell from his nose.

The chipmunk, meanwhile, had disappeared.

# Investigative Reporting

Leland and Merlin weren't the only ones on the track of a killer. Back at the office, the ladies were also discussing matters.

"I'd like to do a little background on the victims of our killer," Nancy Gillis told Ruth, "and I want use the Sheriff's computer."

Ruth rolled her eyes upwards. "That's a departmental data base in that computer and only to be used on official business. Which means, by a '*departmental official*'.

"Whatever I find out, you'd be welcome to."

"Isn't *that* big of you," Ruth scoffed.

"What you don't seem to *get*, little woman," Ruth continued, after Nancy refused to walk away, "is that this (she patted the computer tower) is *proprietary* information. Which means that it is the property of a *Department* of the United States Government, a *Federal* database used by *this Bureau*, which can only be accessed by someone who has the proper *occupational* clearance."

"I *knew* you would be the most likely person to hold a *clearance*," Nancy replied with evident awe.

Ruth bathed in this for a moment.

"For *some* things. The Sheriff holds the passwords for other, more sensitive areas. But none of those people include you, young lady." Ruth riveted Nancy with a look.

"But the victims are dead. And I don't see how any of this covers the killer. I mean, what is there about our killer that you don't want me to find out? " Nancy implored Ruth.

Ruth shook her head.

"Why not think about it this way Ms. Haphelstot? Aren't there a lot of things about this case that *you* would like to know, and that *might* help in the investigation if *we* could dig them up? You would like to do that wouldn't you, Ms. Haphelstot? Help with the investigation? And myself, I understand computers probably better than anyone here because… I'm *young*. Everybody knows that."

"It's true," Ramey said. "I've got a *ten year old* who helps me out at the office."

Ruth was chewing on a painted fingernail. "Well. There *are* a few questions of my *own*, I've had about these murders. Which Sheriff Leland hasn't had the time or the inclination I'm unhappy to say, to pursue. And I can't seem to figure out the data base."

Nancy could tell that Ruth really wanted to allow it.

"Go ahead. Let the girl try her luck," Ms. Loomis, the Muffin Lady, said over whatever it was Ramey was saying. "I'd be interested in what the government could tell me about myself that I don't already know."

"See. So we've got one dead person already who doesn't care. Or, who actually *wants to know*." Nancy nodded briskly.

"At the office," Ramey shouted, after snapping his head hard. Nancy imagined perhaps this tossed the Muffin Lady clear of his thoughts or at least to the side. "My ten year old often opens confidential accounts in order to repair things. There's no other way around it, unless I were to endanger treatment. So I just make him swear to non-disclosure. And we treat it that way."

"You made a ten year old swear to non-disclosure?" Ruth frowned.

"On a deck of baseball cards. He takes it very seriously."

"Wait a minute. I'm a reporter," Nancy interjected. "How can I report what I'm not allowed to disclose?"

"Good point," Ruth said. "That might work."

"Not for me," Nancy protested. "What do I get out of it?"

"You get the information. You just can't attribute it to this source." Ramey's head snapped back sharply the other direction, as the Muffin Lady interjected. "Trust me. I've done lots of interviews, and that's how it works. And once you have the information, it's usually easy to find another source. For example, say you find out I once lived in Cincinnati. Then you go to the Cincinnati data base and see if I'm located there. And when you file your story you just say, 'According to the public files in the data base of the Cincinnati Better Business Bureau, Mary Loomis previously owned and operated a shop called "Tasty Muffins" there from 1985-1987.' You see, simple."

"Is that true?" Nancy asked. "You're from Cincinatti?"

"Pretty much."

"C'mon," Ramey urged. "We all want out of here. The sooner we crack this case the better for all concerned."

Everybody nodded, including eventually Ruth, who sighed. "Oh alright," she said, lifting her newly polished nails from the keyboard and allowing Nancy her seat. "Let's do something!"

# Tracking a Scent

"Do you know that Robert Frost poem, where he says,

"Two roads diverged in a wood, and I--
I took the one less traveled by," ?

Nancy spoke as her fingers raced over the keyboard.

"Well, Mr. Wallace, the teacher I had for investigative journalism, said that you find those 'two roads'? And you trace them back to where they first 'diverged'? And that will make 'all the difference'."

Nancy had supplanted Ruth at the keyboard and was speaking to the others clustered around as she sped her investigation through the networked maze of a national data base. Nancy had two files open.

"Okay. In this window I'm back tracing our first victim, Clarisse Clemens. Oh, this is interesting. She has past arrests for prostitution and confidence games."

"She could've met any kind of murdering low lifes in those professions," Ramey suggested.

"I've never done *any* of those things," the Muffin Lady objected sharply.

"Okay. By 'interesting', I meant that her background will add color to the article." Nancy turned and smiled.

Ramey smiled sweetly back. 'This is weird,' Nancy shuddered.

"Anyway," Nancy said, "so in this other window I'm tracing Ms. Loomis here, our 'Muffin Lady'. Oh, look at all the articles here. And here's those two of mine in the New York Times! The first with the picture of Sheriff Leland, and then the second with those pictures and story of the shoot out..."

"And! moving on..." Ruth said.

"Sorry," Nancy apologized.

"You know, I don't believe I've seen anyone test the Sheriff more than you have little girl," Ruth admonished her.

"I know, I know. I'm sorry," Nancy apologized again. "Mr. Wallace said that we may have to say that a lot. But that, that was *okay*, as long as we did our job. We got the story," she said a little more upbeat.

"Remind me to have a word or two with this Mr. Wallace of yours," Ruth said.

Nancy kept her head down and continued searching through the screens trying this keyword, then that; this association, then that.

This went on for several hours. Nancy kept at it, while Ruth stepped outside to have a smoke. Then Ramey walked back to his cell to lie down and cover his eyes with a cool washcloth. Then Ruth stepped back inside and phoned across the street for some take out lunch. Then they all ate while staring at the screen. By the late afternoon Ramey was sawing logs while Ruth was playing solitaire in the Sheriff's office.

"I've got it!" Nancy cried. "You were born in Pinch, West Virginia. Doctor Ramey. Doctor Ramey! Did you hear that?"

"I could have *told* you that had you just asked!" Ramey/Muffin Lady spoke groggily.

"And Clarisse Clemens was born in Charleston but raised in Elkview, West Virginia," Nancy declared.

"Yeah. Just a few miles up the holler," the Muffin Lady called from the back cell.

"Quite a coincidence, huh?" Nancy exclaimed. "Maybe you two went to the same school?"

"No. No. The kids from Elkview attended Milton middle school and then later on went on to Benton High. While we went to the local Pinch Middle School, and then attended Sadie Meyers High. We only saw them at the games. And me, rarely, because girls didn't have any sports, and I'd be damned if I was going to go miles out of my way to scream and cheer for a bunch of pimpled boys who felt any recognition opened the door to my drawers."

"Oh." Nancy reddened slightly. "Well, still, you have to admit.

This is an enormous coincidence."

" But that's all it is." Ruth nodded.

"What do you mean?!"

"That's all it is. It is *maybe* a large coincidence. But that's *all*," Ruth said. "What, if anything, does this tell us?"

"Jeeze." Nancy sighed, and turned back to the computer. "You know, you people in law enforcement don't get enthused enough. Maybe you should get out more Ruth. Shoot something," she groused.

It took Nancy three more days of after school sleuthing, before she finally hit upon it.

Sheriff Leland and Merlin had returned meanwhile with their news. And the Sheriff had beaten up the phone and hammered on the computer for several days himself trying to figure out just who Bob and Harriet Weeds had fed to the pigs. He tried all the databases. He used all his passwords. Then Agent Hailey dipped into her FBI database using all her passwords. Ruth Googled. And Merlin went back to his vet lab to see what he could find and match with the weird plastic shred of evidence they had. But they all drew blanks. "What in the world good is an ID, if the agency doesn't exist?" Merlin asked.

"Probably just for show," Leland admitted.

"So they could have been just anybody, posing to be anybody?" Merlin said.

Leland sighed, and laughed ruefully.

"We might have well just spoken to the pigs," Merlin declared.

Leland smiled.

"I've got it!" Nancy squealed from Ruth's office.

Both Leland and Merlin's brows rose. "What have you got?" Leland called from his office.

"Just... the *answer!*" Nancy called haughtily.

# The Muffin Lady's Secret

"Look at this," Nancy nodded, when Sheriff Leland and veterinarian Merlin stepped into the room. "Here it is, in the Charleston Gazette, October 23rd, 1986":

## Girls Civics Club Bus Goes Missing for 6 Hours

A school bus carrying eight girls to the School Government and Civics Symposium in Charleston went missing for 6 hours yesterday, school authorities have reported. The girls were from the communities of Pinch and Elkview, West Virginia. The twelve mile trip, which should have taken about one hour, took seven hours instead. Neither the driver nor any of the students on the bus had any explanation, saying that they believed it had been just a normal drive. They were a little puzzled they said, when they arrived in Charleston around sundown and glanced at their watches. But otherwise, they could recount nothing unusual as having occurred, nor did they feel any ill effects except "having missed lunch, apparently".

Authorities meanwhile are interrogating the driver, checking the bus odometer and asking local residents to call if they could report having seen this bus anytime between the hours of 11am and 5pm yesterday.

"Did you happen to be on that bus?" Sheriff Leland asked Ramey, who happened to be in the nature of Nancy Loomis then.

Ms. Loomis read the article one more time, then placed Ramey's palms to his head and sat down.

"Was Clarisse Clemens on that bus?" Leland asked.

"I don't know. We got on. We had never met with the other girls, so we sat with our own friends. And then, after we arrived in Charleston, it was so weird, my parents came and got me and we drove home."

"About two weeks later, I started having dreams," Ms. Loomis continued. The Muffin Lady pressed Ramey's fingertips to his forehead. "About nothing I'd ever seen and being in other peoples' bodies…" She glanced at Ramey's hands and looked in her pocket mirror at Ramey's face. "Oh my God," she said.

"You never told a soul about all this?" Ruth asked in disbelief.

"About my *dreams*?" The Muffin Lady laughed harshly.

Leland shook his head.

Then Ramey spoke. "Where'd she go?" He asked.

"Who?" Ruth asked.

"That business woman. The Muffin Lady." Ramey glanced around as if she had been in the room standing right beside him.

Ruth's glasses slipped off her nose.

# Opening Night Jitters

Ralph Bunch still didn't feel quite himself Thursday morning as he hung his show in the back room of the Campaign Café. He'd tried calling the Everlee's to see if they could postpone the unveiling of the prize Guernsey till next month, but Cynthia Everlee had pleaded with him to try and finish. It was to be for George Everlee's fiftieth birthday and people were driving from some distance to attend. So under deadline Ralph was still painting as it hung on the wall. He'd been up all night and the past day and drinking coffee mixed with a little Three Feathers Whiskey. In his flurry of activity, he was smearing and dribbling paint across the floor and walls but still couldn't get the heifer's head at all right - in fact, not even close to …cow.

It was a matter of likeness - the lowest of all aesthetic indicators to an artist, but one of the highest to a patron Ralph knew. It kept looking like a squirrel! Or maybe it just 'felt' like a squirrel. Ralph didn't know. Whatever it was, Ralph just couldn't hit it on the sweet spot where everything felt done and… well, Guernsey-like! 'For Pete's sake!' Ralph berated himself, 'You *ought* to know Guernseys.'

Ralph walked backwards with his eyes squinted. Then he walked forwards with his eyes squinted, and then extra wide open, and then completely shut and then squinted again and made an adjustment - all the while nibbling nuts. Which was the problem really. He didn't nibble nuts. He didn't like nuts! Maybe. He didn't know. Though he'd *thought* he knew. Just like he'd *thought* he knew Guernseys. He seemed to be in some netherworld between familiar landmarks.

His mind was *uncomfortable*, like it was a trying to park a bus, or to navigate down a twisting alley while seated sideways in the driver's seat. 'Damn!' He was losing - or had lost - his ability to *feel* Guernsey.

With this realization came an electric bolt of fear running from his bottommost chakra right up his backbone like a high voltage line causing him to pitch the brush.

Losing the ability to think Guernsey in dairy country could be catastrophic! *He was going to starve and then to die - cold and alone, maybe even sober - unheralded and forgotten.* Every struggling artist fears at some point that this will happen. "And if it has to happen, then it will happen." That's what the Realists all say. Ralph Bunch had tried his best, until now, to sidestep the inevitable.

But it was a lot harder once it had happened.

Still, he fought back with his own mental jujitsu. After all, he reasoned. I don't paint reality. I paint an illusion. Let reality deal with itself, and I'll continue painting. This life's strategy of his had worked so far.

With his spirits so buoyed, even so shakily, he sucked down some more coffee and shut his eyes tight. Then opened them. He must have painted 500 Guernseys in this life. He scrabbled across the floor and gripped the brush tight. He could do one more.

# Leland's Love Jitters

Leland, meanwhile, was having his own problems. He had tried asking Agent Hailey out. He had begun, "Agent Hailey?"

"Yes," she said.

"I was won..."

Leland looked at Agent Hailey, who appeared barely awake. She was all tired efficiency and probably held upright only by her stiff uniform. They'd all been pushing themselves pretty hard.

"Gee, you look bushed. We need a night off," he declared finally.

"Serial killers don't take nights off," Agent Hailey replied, rather rote like.

"Well, we don't know that, do we? And they certainly should," Leland declared.

Agent Hailey just looked at him. He thought she might be going to say something dismissive, but instead, her eyes closed. Just as she opened her mouth to speak, she fell directly forward, her head stuck in Leland's stomach, where she lay passed out and snoring softly.

Leland rousted Ramey out of the cell and lay Agent Hailey on the bunk. Then he turned off the light and shut the inside door so that she could get some uninterrupted sleep.

When Agent Hailey awoke it was about 6 pm, and Leland suggested they get some dinner at the Café "...across the way, and then maybe catch some of the local culture. What do you think?" He added, his eye twitching.

Agent Hailey looked around the darkened cell, and then at Sheriff Leland groggily, like a child being awakened in the depths of the night and told they had to leave right away for 'somewhere'. "Okay," she mumbled.

But she wasn't entirely present until around twenty minutes later when she studied, with some of her old presence, the crowd in the Café and the meatloaf and potatoes with homemade gravy which had been placed before her. "What's with the crowd?" Agent Hailey asked, staring at the plate instead of the crowd.

"They're gathering for Culture Night," Leland responded.

"Sheriff Kelly. May I call you 'Leland'?" Agent Hailey asked.

"I wish you would." Leland smiled.

"Leland," Agent Hailey began again, licking some of the sleepy drool from her lower lip with a finger and taking a sip of coffee." "What the hell is 'Culture Night'?"

"You remember the artist I told you about who painted the cell you just finished sleeping in?"

"Yes."

"His name is Ralph Bunch. His family has lived around here for ages. But I'd say he's the only 'artist' they've ever sprouted. And his specialty is painting scenes from hereabouts, most notably cows and such. And every month he has a showing. He covers the walls of the bar in back. And he often recites a small poem or squib of something he's composed while in the midst of creating his paintings. So far I'd guess I've heard everything which could ever be said about Guernseys. Each month I'd be willing to wager it, but each month, Ralph proves me wrong." Leland smiled. "Actually," he added, "it's called *Poetry Night*." Leland spoke this latter with a lift of his fork and knife and a little flourish.

"That's real romantic." Agent Hailey nodded, several times, as if thinking that - and her meatloaf with homemade gravy - over.

"Agent Hailey," Leland set his silverware to ask, later. "May I call you....?"

"Yes?"

"You've never told me your first name."

"Agent."

"Agent?" Leland looked confused, and then a little disheartened.

"Hey!" Agent Hailey poked him with her fork and then stole a bite of his pie. "May name is Suzanne. Suzanne Hailey," she said with a smile. "You were right about their pie. This is really good."

She went for another bite as Leland pulled it away.

"Get your own." Leland smiled.

For the rest of the meal they chattered like two high school seniors.

# Poetry Night

Leland saw that the crowd was beginning to move into the back room. So he paid their bill and while Agent Hailey went to 'freshen up', he told her he'd step into the bar and grab them some good stools.

Actually, the back room was larger than your normal bar. This was because it was sometimes used to host dances and meetings. Varnished wood lined the room. There were hard liquor signs. (Carmella said Peter felt neon beer signs were 'cheap', 'looked rural', and 'lacked class'.) There was a small stage also. And that's where Ralph was nervously toying with the amped microphone - with the usual "Test, test, testing…" and squeals. Some folding chairs had been set up.

Above, and around, the bar there were the usual stuffed heads of the critters shot around the area, not excluding the stuffed heads of a pig and a Guernsey cow. This usually got a guffaw from whatever tourist happened by and usually the extra drink order as they contemplated it. And maybe an extra drink for a local as they spun a yarn about it. Making up a yarn about the "Cow on the Wall" to retail outsiders with was considered local fun.

Leland saw two free seats and grabbed them. He sat in the chair nearest a short, stocky fireplug of a guy finishing a shot of liquor. They guy gave him no notice but immediately ordered another. He looked up when it arrived and the bright bar light must have immediately initiated a sneeze…

"Oh fuck, oh goddamn, oh goddamn," the man cried as he inhaled, and then, "Fuuuuuuuuckkkkkkk!" As he sneezed, wincing and tearing up with the pain. "Fuck, fuck, fuck, fuck!" He exclaimed gripping the bar till his pain ebbed. "Shit," he said, seeing that his whiskey had spilled.

"Gesundheit," Leland offered.

"And fuck your gesundheit, too," the man snarled, not glancing back.

Leland considered this, then nodded, and resumed his thoughts regarding Agent Hailey. 'Suzanne', she had said. Leland smiled.

Somewhere between the beer bubbles, Suzanne and he were in the tropics. Leland's fruity drink was ice cold. A gently breeze played with Suzanne's hair. They were lying back on identical blue chaise loungers staring out at the sea with their weapons lying on the cabana table between them, cleaned and ready for use.

"You're the Sheriff, aren't you?" The fireplug demanded of the bar mirror.

Leland considered this. In his pleasant thoughts both of them were reaching as if in synchronous motion for their weapons with a quick, clean sweep of their arms.

"Well, either you are, or you aren't." The man shook his head with disgust.

Leland spoke back to the mirror. "I'm guessing someone broke your ribs by the way you reacted to that sneeze. I've experienced a couple broken ribs myself, so I know what *that* feels like. And I'm guessing you didn't get kicked by a cow, since you don't smell like manure. Most people with their ribs broken that aren't yelling at a cow in a field are talking to the Sheriff in kind of a pissed off way because they had them broken by someone else, another human, because no one has ever asked me to arrest a cow." Leland sized the fellow up. Aside from the spark plug tattoo on his arm, which Leland liked, he couldn't say he cared much for the fellow. The guy just made an awful first impression and Leland wouldn't have minded giving him a jab in the ribcage himself. "But this is just from my experience as your Sheriff. I am assuming you're from here. How am I doing?" Leland asked the mirror.

The man turned to face Leland. "Nobody told me our Sheriff was a smartass."

"That's good to hear." Leland nodded. "What's on your mind?"

"You've got a psycho loose in your town, in case you don't know it."

"I'd say that's pretty much common knowledge." Leland

nodded.

"I don't mean *that* psycho. I mean *this* psycho." The man pointed at his ribs.

"You've still got your head?" Leland asked.

"Just barely!" The man exclaimed. "The guy had his knife out."

"Uh?" Leland became a little more interested.

"Yeah. ...Uh!" The man acted as if Leland couldn't hear. Leland leaned back. "Then that psycho shut his eyes, made a deep sigh - as if trying to *restrain* himself - and put it away. I tell you. I thought I was a goner. I thought I was about to be *dissected*. ...Oh shit!" The man exclaimed, thinking to stifle another sneeze. But it was a false alarm.

"Where did this happen?" Leland asked, moving his beer so that the man wouldn't sneeze into it.

"Right in back. Here!" The man had a way of phrasing everything as if the person he was speaking to were an idiot.

"In back of the restaurant?"

"You're kind of slow aren't you? Yeah! Right in back *here*, in back of the restaurant."

"What were you doing back there?"

"What was *I* doing back there? I'm the cook, for Godsakes! Who do you think prepares your damned food?"

Leland just nodded. "Okay. I see." Leland smiled. "It's just that I'm really surprised someone would ever want to insult or perish the thought, hurt a *cook*." Leland laughed. "How did this come about?" Leland folded his hands, all ears.

The man regarded Leland.

"You don't give a fuck, do you?" The man said loudly enough so that others turned.

"No," Leland replied softly with an edge to his voice. "Actually, I'm beginning to give it a real personal concern." He made as if to rearrange the man's coat on the back of his chair with his left hand, while manipulating the man's broken ribs with two stiff fingers of his right.

"Oooooh fuck, fuck, fuckkkkkkkk!" The man squinted and cried, real tears.

People were turned and looking. Leland put his arm even more protectively around the man's shoulder and spoke softly, as if consoling the man beneath the bar noise while handing him a paper napkin. Leland smiled at the other patrons. "Just one of the stages of grief." Several nodded hesitantly and turned away.

"Look," Leland said quietly. "One of the rules of being a small town Sheriff is that if I take shit from any one, then I'm not the alpha dog. And I *have* to be the alpha dog. Otherwise the whole social fabric is torn. Total chaos ensues. Do you understand this?" Leland screwed his left index and middle knuckles into the man's ribs.

"Yeeeessss!" The man cried.

Leland handed him another tissue and patted him on the back. "You're a reasonable man."

The man rose to leave. Leland restrained him.

"There's more," Leland said, setting him back down.

Leland waited. The man nodded.

"Now I'm going to ask you a few questions, and you're going to give me clear answers. Okay?"

"Okay."

Leland asked.

The man replied. "He's another cook here! I stepped out to take a break, and saw him sitting there on the back stoop. I told him to get back to work. He told me he didn't want to. So I got in his face a little."

Leland nodded. "And what happened then?"

"He..." The man struggled with his hands to describe it. "...had me on my back with my ribs stomped in before I could whistle. I never even seen it coming. The man's as fast as shit. And then, I was looking up at him with his knife out."

"Okay," Leland said. "And then?"

"Then he decides to go back inside and continue cooking. That's it. I picked myself up and took the day off. I went home."

"So you run the kitchen?"

"Not anymore." The man nodded to where another man was standing. "*He* does."

Leland glanced that way. "What do the others have to say about this? It sounds like he's new."

"He is," the man spoke into the bar mirror. "That is, he was the newest, up until a while ago. But no one says a word against him. All that fella has to do is to mumble, at *any* of them, and the shit dribbles right outta their shorts." The man asked for another shot.

Leland considered this. "What about Carmella?" He asked. "I can't see Carmella putting up with that."

The man looked at Leland like he was hopeless.

"He's the one who's knocking her!" The man replied. "You can't hear it?!" He regarded Leland with scorn. "Are you deaf?" He shook his head.

"I had my secretary close the window," Leland replied.

"Yeah, I'd guess." The fellow replied, sullenly. "You hear one of Carmella's screams, I suppose you've heard them all. It can really grate on you, you know? Especially when you're trying to plan the next weeks work schedule."

Leland regarded his beer for a while. He had some more questions he could ask. But frankly, he didn't want to talk with the fellow any longer. So he took his arm from around the man's shoulders. "You can go now." He nodded.

"Go. Why do I have to go? I'm staying right here."

Leland gave him a look and had to shake his head at the man's damned contrariness.

"You want to press charges?" Leland asked, looking again at the man the Sparkplug had indicated.

"Yeah! After he's dead *and* buried." Sparky laughed, speaking all this into the mirror and refusing to glance at the man or Leland again. "At *least* six feet down and *two* weeks after."

Leland sat ruminating on this while the Sparkplug remained right where he was.

"I guess this makes us friends now then," Leland said, seeing as how the fellow hadn't left.

"I don't have any friends," the man replied.

Leland nodded. Then he did his best to observe the stranger through the mirror without spooking the guy.

# Things Get Squirrely

Agent Hailey arrived about the time things got going.

More chairs had been set out. Most of the Everlees and their friends had arrived. From the silence it sounded as though Ralph Bunch had gotten the microphone feedback solved. Behind the microphone, hung in the place of honor and covered in black velvet, was the commissioned painting.

"George Everlee's prize Guernsey won the Kimmel County Milkers Association *Producer of the Year* Award, and has done this three years running," Leland told Agent Hailey. "She's quite a woman."

"I imagine." Agent Hailey smiled.

"So they've had her portrait commissioned. The Association is thinking of having this done for each of the yearly winners, to be hung in a place as yet to be determined. So this reception is a big night for Ralph. That might be why he appears so nervous."

"Or it could be that he's always been a screw-up and a loser and that preys upon his confidence," Leland's sour new acquaintance to the left said.

Leland leaned to his left. "You're going to sit here with your mouth zipped shut for the rest of the evening - or I'm going to smack you in the ribs so hard with my elbow that you'll see spots," Leland told his new acquaintance. "Would you like another tissue?"

"I can keep my mouth shut," the man said.

"Okay."

Leland nodded towards where Ralph was chewing peanuts. He looked as if he were struggling with a compulsion to eat, first pushing the bowl of peanuts away - then pulling it back. He appeared quite conflicted. "He doesn't look quite himself tonight," he noted to Agent Hailey. "Ralph is an odd duck. I think I'll go up and have a chat with him." He smiled at Agent Hailey and excused himself. "And don't you even *glance* at her," Leland said to the man on his right. The man's eyes, which had been wandering over Agent Hailey snapped forward.

Leland walked up to Ralph. "Ralph, how're you doing?" Leland settled, reaching to take a peanut from the bowl.

"Don't touch those." Ralph pulled them away.

Leland laughed.

Ralph's head shot forward and Leland jerked back instinctively. It looked like Ralph had tried to bite him!

"What the hell, Ralph?" Leland stood, taking a step backwards.

"Don't touch my fucking nuts!"

"Okay," Leland said. "I'll leave your junk alone."

Ralph studied Leland, as if Leland were up to something he didn't comprehend.

"You pretty nervous, huh? This time around?"

"Oh Leland, you don't know. My career is over. My life is probably nearing its end."

This seemed more like the overly sensitive Ralph that Leland knew. Leland sat down. He nodded to Agent Hailey to indicate that this might take a moment.

"I can't paint anymore!" Ralph whispered into Leland's ear.

Leland furrowed his brows.

"All it seems I can do is to chew and harbor nuts, like a squirrel," Ralph sputtered.

Leland reached unconsciously for another peanut as he listened. And Ralph flew at his arm with his teeth.

"Shit!" Leland exclaimed, shoving Ralph off. There was drool left on his shirt. Ralph's teeth probably would have broken the skin if it hadn't been for the tough fabric. "What the hell?"

"I can't control it!" Ralph cried, eyes wide. "I tried to warn you."

"Control what?"

"I don't know. The *mind*, I think, of the chipmunk." Ralph had his ten fingertips to his scalp as if to help him focus far off on some vision. "He's so.... *feral.*"

Leland nodded.  Leland decided Ralph had been better left alone.

Leland walked back to the bar.  Agent Hailey asked, "What's wrong with Ralph?  Did he try to *bite* you?"

"I don't know." Leland shook his head.  "I hope it's not rabies." Leland wiped the saliva from his shirt sleeve with a bar napkin.  "He was going on about some chipmunk."

"This might not have been the best night for you to have attended.  But I feel now, like I'd better stay and watch over things," Leland added.  "You want to go?"

"No." Agent Hailey frowned, swirling the straw in her drink.  "I want to hear about that chipmunk.  He sounds questionable, like an up and comer.  Perhaps I should be carrying."

"Yeah." Leland frowned.

Finally, it came time for the ceremony to begin.

# ...and Squirrellier

As Leland and Agent Hailey settled back with their drinks, Ralph began.

"Good evening." Ralph gave a hesitant smile.

"Good evening, Ralph!" Someone called, to a titter of laughter.

Ralph nodded. "I hope so," he began tentatively.

"Just show us the painting!" That someone called.

"Shut up!" Someone else called.

The commissioned painting was hung directly behind Ralph and covered in black velvet. It was quite large as befitted a fifteen hundred dollar commission.

"As you know," Ralph began again.

"Speak up!"

"Shut up!"

"As you know! Ralph leaned too close to the microphone.

"*!*!***!!!!!" The feedback jarred everyone in the room.

Ralph jerked back and hesitated as if he were afraid to go near the mike again. This brought another titter of laughter. Ralph gazed out over his audience with saucer-sized eyes, and a hand dove for the peanuts. He stood their cracking and eating several with saucer-sized eyes, while his audience sat, waiting.

Finally, with both cheeks full of nuts, Ralph approached the microphone again, carefully, as if he couldn't understand the thing. "As you know," he said. "I am primarily a painter of rural, and that is in our case, agricultural settings." Though with all of the nuts in his cheeks this came out a little more like, "ur his hin hower cashe , hagghricalshurrrel *shittings*." This last got a laugh. Ralph swallowed and drank some water.

"But fine artists down through history have not only reveled in depicting how their friends and neighbors earned their living, but felt it their duty to celebrate it in song, story and painting."

George Everlee nodded and started the applause. "Farmers are the backbone of this community," he called out. "And we owe it mostly to just a great breed of Guernsey we have developed right here - in Kimmel County!"

There were lots of cheers; even fist pumps.

Ralph nodded. "Praise the Lord for our abundance," he said.

"Yes. Yes. Yes," it was murmured around the room.

"Are we in a tavern here, or are we in a church?" A heckler shouted.

"Shut up!!!" Was the widespread response.

"As you know also, from my other times up here, that I believe 'Wherever the Lord has brought abundance, the Devil views jealously." Ralph's eyes narrowed.

The room was quiet.

"Wherever His Good Works Are In Evidence, the Devil plots." Ralph's voice dropped and paused.

"Ah yes. Yea, yea, yea," some in the audience responded. Others began to sway, ( from drink.).

"And WHEREEVER the Good Lord Savior *most* blesses, THERE is where old Beezlebub most seeks to leave his brand!" Ralph's eyes bugged, and his elbows locked as he held the mike.

Hands were lifted.

But not George Everlee's. George Everlee was smiling stiffly, not looking around, while his wife Arlene fought, inconspicuously, to get Ralph's attention. But Ralph's eyeballs were by now surely big as eggs and the veins in his temple bulged.

"George Everlee's Guernsey, Daffodil, was surely most blessed," Ralph continued, pointing to the cloth covered painting with a nod to Ralph Everlee.

Ralph Everlee smiled, relaxed a bit and nodded tentatively.

"Why I can still remember that frosty morning she was first delivered," Ralph said. "I was working on another portrait of a sort in a far part of the barn of Henrietta, George's prize sow. Many of you, of a few year's memory, surely remember her. I've got to say, she had the best flesh tones of any sow I've had the pleasure yet to paint in this area... mostly yellow ochre and Old Holland white with

175

just the barest highlight of vermillion."

Arlene blushed.  But George nodded emphatically and pumped his fist to a general cheer which arose from the crowd.  "It's *Stumps Magic Sow Cream!*" for any of you who are interested!"  George called out.

Ralph nodded, then moved closer to the mike.

"I know many of you here now - right now - have either laughed slightly, or just coughed, when you have heard me say up here in the past that an Artist has to Beat the Devil each time he takes up his brush.  That Art is so important to the glorification of God that the Devil must see to it *himself*, that this process we call *Creation* and lent to us by God Himself - goes awry - so that what is meant to be a glorification *instead* becomes an *abom-min-nation.*"  Ralph leaned on this last word as if to squeeze all the sin from it.

Arlene looked worried.  And Ralph Everlee and his kin, nestled nervously around, clearly were wondering where this was all headed.  There was a nervous reaching for drinks.

"I think you'd better just show us the painting, Ralph," the voice in the back called.

And this time it was answered by a murmured chorus of assents.

"Before he does!"  Arlene Everlee stood up, bravely trying to turn the river of some dark destiny to which it seemed Fate had deemed course through their celebratory evening.  "I just want to say how proud I am of my husband George and his prize Guernsey Daffodil!  And for the honor he has bestowed upon all of us here this evening who are gathered to toast our profession.  And I just want to add," as she teared up, "that George has been as good a husband and provider these twenty-five years as he is a breeder and Daffodil is a milker."

"Hear!  Hear!"  Voices cried.

They all drank to that, while Arlene blubbered and George Everlee kissed her.

"Show us the painting for Godsakes, Ralph," many shouted.

"Well, to paraphrase Kris Kristofferson, I'm not going to say I beat the Devil," Ralph said, gripping a corner of the drapery. "But I drank his beer for free."

Inwardly Leland cringed.

Ralph pulled the curtain free.

"…and then I painted his Face."

Ralph had gotten most of the prize Guernsey, Daffodil, right excepting for the head, which resembled exactly that of a huge chipmunk's.

A gasp rose up.

Silence gripped the room, while everyone fought to realize what to think, and then, whether or not to say it - and turned generally towards George Everlee whose jaw had fallen near to the floor. It was George's herd manager, Earl, who finally spoke.

"Well…. he got her *tits* right," he remarked gruffly.

# Aftermath

"I hope you haven't paid that bastard anything yet," George Everlee swore.

"Now dear, I think it's best we don't decide anything just yet. Let's go home. Tomorrow's another day. We can talk more about it then, after a good night's sleep and a little time to reflect."

"You're probably right," George agreed. "All of my guns are at home, and I've probably drunk too much to hit anything square."

Arlene made a mental note to hide all of George's guns, once he was asleep and in bed.

Ralph, meanwhile, had returned to drink. He'd finished off his first bottle of Three Feathers Whiskey and was well into his second.

"The troubhle his, withtha nose," Ralph slurred, waving his arm dismissively at Daffodils portrait, "With a portrait hits hallways tha nhosh*e*!" Ralph grabbed the arm of a man nearest, who had been studying the painting closely, pulling him in. "You cahn't mhake 'um happy! It's heither too lahrge  whore too schmall… whore too thish whore too that. Hits nehver  jhust  rhight!!!" Ralph stated.

The man happened to be Stan.

"So that *chipmunk* really got into your head, eh?" Stan asked, studying the painting and then Ralph intently. He looked very interested. Perhaps he was an art lover, Ralph thought.

"Hew chould shay as much." Ralph nodded. "Hi can't hear him. But hi can *feheel* him hall hover hinside! HIt's like he's ruhmmaging haround in there meshing with mhe." Ralph grabbed Stan's wrist. "What I want, what I hintended to dho …"

"Kinda make you want to strangle the little fucker, eh!" Stan's brows rose, as he examined the chipmunk's face again.

"Hi don't know. Hive nhever wanted to schtrangle anything? Hide have to think about hit," Ralph mused.

"But you'd like to kill it if you could, wouldn't you?  Maybe poke around inside it skull, see how it works? How it does what it's doing?" Stan insisted.

"Hi don't know. Hi would kind of like to find a way to *talk* to it, if I could. Mahybe bhe friends." Ralph nodded.

Stan shook his head. "Be friends. Talk to it," he muttered.

"Buht hit doeshn't scheem to tahlk! Hit's mohre lihke hit buhrrowed hinto mihe mihdbrain, whore something," Ralph reflected.

Stan had disappeared.

Leland glanced around from speaking with Agent Hailey and the new cook was gone. "You see where our 'psycho' went?" Leland asked.

"Who me?" Sparkplug man replied into the mirror. "The guy who's been trying real hard to just stare straight ahead?"

"Somehow or other I am going to find a good excuse to punch you real hard in the ribs again." Leland shook his head.

He walked over to speak with Ralph.

"Don't bite me Ralph." Leland cautioned. "I harbor no interest in your bowl of peanuts."

"Hi nehver meahnt to bhite yyou, Lehland." A tear ran down Ralph's cheek. "That's hall what hi have bheen shaying! Hits that damn chipmunk." Ralph gestured at the painting with his raised drink. "She mhade mhe dho hit. *The Dehvil mhade mhe dho hit!*" Ralph bawled.

Leland nodded. "Speaking of the Devil. Who was that fellow you were just talking too, *now*?" Leland asked.

"Who? Him?..." Ralph glanced around. "Hi dohn't know. Juhst a rheal nhice fhellow hart lohver. Lehland. Dhidn't look lhike a Dhemocraht. Buht he saihdt, he felht mhi *pain*. Whore mahbe hi jhust himferred hit." Ralph searched for words. "Dho *yyou* hunderstand what his happening haround here, Lehland?"

"No, I don't understand Ralph. I don't understand it at *all*. But, I'm working on it." Leland patted his arm.

"How are you doing?" Agent Hailey asked.

Leland thought it might be permissible to squeeze Agent Hailey's shoulder as he sat down beside her on his return. She didn't resist.

"It seems the evening has crashed, and your painter friend over there is in tears." She looked concerned.

"Ah!" Leland waved her concerns away. "Ralph's been kicked when he's down before. That's the thing you get to know about Ralph. He's not too good in the stand-up sort of way, but boy can he endure. He's like moss or paint, or *shit*, when I consider it. Stepping in it… just makes it spread. Ralph will find a way to make hay of this catastrophe. He's nothing if not creative. Moss can find a way to make a pleasant enough situation of wherever it finds itself, even on gravestones. Ralph is like that."

"There's a dark but practical sentiment."

Leland shrugged.

"I know the next person we need to talk to," he said.

# A Positive ID

Stan really wanted inside the Kimmel jail. Something itched, and as near as Stan could triangulate that fifty year old weathered yellow jail was at the nub of it. It was interfering with his sex. Something in that jail was a 'scold'. That was the best way he could phrase it, if he were to talk to someone about it, like a psychiatrist, which he couldn't.

Then, as luck would have it, apparently Stan's Kandahar Omelet was a hit with the Sheriff. Ruth had called Carmella with her usual breakfast order that Sunday and asked, "Could you have the cook who makes that delicious curry-egg concoction bring it over himself? I want to finagle that recipe out of him, if I can."

Or so this was the story. When you're wanted for rapes and serial murders, you really tend to look several times at any approach especially when made by law enforcement personnel. On the other hand, Stan preened, it was true that his Kandahar Omelet *had* made a little culinary noise even in the sleepy town of Kimmel. Partly it was because he was a veteran, he knew. But it *also* sold well. So it was with some unfulfilled professional yearning that Stan laid each of the cooked bacon strips neatly on a paper towel, then cracked eggs and dropped them in the bacon grease to cook while he considered the request seriously.

Stan flipped the eggs. None of the yolks broke, and as the eggs bubbled in the bacon grease, Stan convinced himself by thinking, 'Look. If I had thought up this scheme *myself*, wouldn't I try it?' Stan hoisted the eggs out, arranged the eggs on the plates with the bacon, toast and hash browns, decorated each with an orange slice and a sprig of parsley and placed them in the window just as Carmella passed to lift them away with a wink and a smile.

It was probably Carmella's look that decided it. You had to remain positive in this life, Stan decided. So Stan heaped up a fine, steaming dish of what he liked to call his 12 Egg Complete with Melted Gruyere Cheese Freeze Dried K Packet Kandahar Mortar, covered it with a checkered cloth, put on a clean and unspotted apron and presented it and himself with a big pot of hot coffee at the jail promptly at 7 am early Monday.

After a few preemptory knocks, and the use of a password Ruth had concocted, the front door opened. "Good morning, Ruth? I'm Stan, the cook from across the way." Stan made no move to enter.

"C'mon in, Stan from across the way." Ruth smiled. "Boy, doesn't that smell good," she said, lifting a corner of the checkered cloth. We all have saved our appetites." She gauged Stan as a slight frown flitted across her face. "Just walk in there and the Sheriff will tell you where to set it. And I'll follow close behind." Stan noticed the young girl reporter from the café working at a computer. He nodded. She seemed to look him over very closely.

Stan smiled his best regular person smile and stepped across the linoleum into the Sheriff's office. "Breakfast?" Leland smiled, looking up and examining Stan. "Could you just set it on the bunk inside that jail cell just next to the one with the prisoner in it?"

Stan hesitated.

Leland raised his brows.

Stan nodded and passed into the jail proper. Stan's brows furrowed, as he passed Ramey, the transvestite, sitting sullenly on his bunk in the other cell. Leland rose and followed behind Stan with Ruth following behind him.

"Ramey, you want some breakfast?" Leland asked. But Ramey sat sullenly staring at Stan, saying nothing.

Stan stared back.

"Cat's probably got his tongue," Leland said.

"You leave his cell door open all the time like that?" Stan nodded.

"This is a converted jail. It used to be a feed store. There are no toilets in the cells. So we have had to come to an understanding. Isn't that right Ramey?" Leland showed a little irritation at Ramey's sudden unwillingness to speak and raised his voice.

"He doesn't talk much either does he?" Stan observed.

Ramey bared his teeth issuing a slight hissss…

"Not at the moment, apparently." Leland frowned. "Why don't you just set the food down in there, and we can see if a little breakfast will lure some conversation out of him."

Stan hesitated to walk into the cell.

Leland urged, hanging onto the swinging iron jail door. "We're right behind. I've got my coffee cup ready. And Ruth's here with her fork and plate." Stan stared at them both.

"Only place with enough seats to fit us all." Leland urged him in.

"What about that young girl? She want some?" Stan asked, back stepping.

"She's already eaten." Leland nodded, blocking his path.

"Ramey, you'd better get over here, you don't want to get left out." Leland turned his head with some real irritation. "Where the hell has Ramey gone?"

"I don't know," Ruth said, turning around herself. "He was in there, just a moment ago."

They both looked befuddled.

They all stood as if in stalemate.

"You run kind of an odd jail here, Sheriff."

"How so?" Leland replied.

"Well," Stan had to laugh. "Your prisoner just walked out the back door there. A small girl is playing on your departmental computer. And the cell here is painted like the waiting room in a bordello." And when this didn't get a rise, he added. "And you two are here looking like you're gonna sit down to eat your breakfast in a jail cell."

"We are." Leland nodded.

"Don't want it to get cold!" Ruth smiled.

"He'll be back," Leland said, settling himself. Leland motioned with his cup.

Stan stood there in wonderment. "Law enforcement people sure are different in a small town," he observed as he poured.

"Oh. How so?" Sheriff Leland smiled. He looked inquisitive. Ruth smiled, too. "Yes. How so?!"

Stan smiled. "Let's eat before it's cold as Afghanistan," he said finally.

Leland nodded. Ruth nodded. As long as they were inside too, Stan decided he'd sit. Everyone ate.

Stan was irritated. He didn't like the way they ate his food. They picked at it, and *pushed it around for Godsakes!* And their comments struck him as perfunctory. They might as well be having oatmeal. Their conversation was inane. No understanding at all of cuisine. And there was nothing special about the jail. That is, the itch he felt, instead of increasing, seemed to have moved away.

Stan asked about the mural, but neither the Sheriff nor his secretary seemed much interested in delving into it, other than to say that Ralph Bunch done it. Stan nodded. "Kind of surprised there's not a chipmunk in it," Stan joked.

"How so?" Leland replied.

"Is that all cops do is ask questions?"

Both of them set their utensils. Stan stared.

The conversation drug. Abruptly Stan cleared the dishes and rose to go. Their prisoner still hadn't returned which was just bizarre. It wasn't even a proper brig! And this irritated Stan more than anything.

Stan was irritated and said so. Which created some uncomfortable moments, when Sheriff Leland said that he didn't care for the omlet so much anyway and Ruth agreed. Both of them staring at him. So that no one saw Ramey enter, passing in through the back door carrying a heavy shovel which he had hoisted over his shoulders like a baseball bat.

Leland returned to his office. Stan had just cleared the cell block while swearing. Ruth was leading the way out, when Ramey, stepping from behind a partition, swung the shovel with all his strength, striking Stan, as he passed, at the base of his skull with a sharp "whang!" Stan went down like a sack of flour.

Ruth turned and gasped.

Leland rushed in with Nancy following.

Ramey dropped the shovel and backed away, looking at them with alarm. "I didn't do it. I didn't do it!" He jumped, shivering with disgust. Nancy wrote this down.

"There's our positive I.D.," Leland said to Ruth, nudging the skull of his suspected serial killer with a toe to better see his face.

Nancy wrote this down.

# Don't Wait for the Movie

"Well," Ruth drawled, in her best hardboiled detective's voice. (Ruth would come to believe that these were her words.) "That is a *positive* ID."

"I'd say so." Leland nodded, removing the cuffs from his belt and placing them on his new prisoner.

"Honest Leland, I didn't do it! I did not do this!" Ramey cried.

"We've figured that Ramey," Ruth consoled him.

"It was this *woman in my head*," Ramey insisted, pointing to his head, then pounding it against the wall. "She's obsessed. And she's *violent*."

"Yeah." Leland nodded and pulled Ramey back from the wall. He grunted as he hefted Stan's bulk upwards so as to get him back into the cell. "My guess is that she figured if she just out and identified our suspect, she'd never get as good a whack at him."

Ruth nodded.

"I don't trust myself around him at all," Ramey admitted, backing away.

They'd just about got the unconscious Stan back into the cell when Ruth said, "Do you smell something Leland?"

Leland sniffed.

"That's natural gas. I mean the kind we use in homes."

Leland stopped dragging Stan and sniffed closer to the floor. He nodded.

"It's collecting down here," he said.

"There's some kind of a gas leak," Ruth agreed.

"We don't have gas service," Leland said.

Leland's lips traced a grim line. "Ramey," he said. "Help me get this prisoner into the Jeep. And Ruth call 911 about a possible gas leak, but warn them it could be an explosive device. Then I want you to drive everyone up to Ramey's house and I'll call Agent Hailey and route her your way."

186

Ruth nodded and ran to make the call. But Leland blocked her path sending her out the back. "On your cell outside," Leland said. "We don't want sparks."

Ruth shook her head and waved her arms, as if to say, "of course! What was I thinking?" She ran out back.

Ramey overcame his reluctance to lift the prisoner - in fact, gripping him so hard around the neck and pulling that his knuckles went white and the prisoners face went blue. Leland had to pull Ramey off and send him down to the prisoner's feet to lift.

Finally Leland and Ramey got the prisoner into the back of the Sheriff's Jeep. Meanwhile, Ruth had made the call and gotten in behind the wheel. Leland smacked the fender. "Okay, now go!"

"What are you going to do?" Ruth asked.

"I'm going out front to clear the street," Leland said.

Ruth nodded , then squirreled away in a spiraling cloud of gravel and dust. 'Without the sirens and lights, please!' Leland thought, but didn't bother to shout knowing it would do as little good. He was already running through the jail and out the front onto Main Street as the wail of a siren reached him. It was morning with its usual smattering of locals mixed in with bunches of tourists.

Within ten minutes Leland had recruited a few of the more responsible townspeople he knew and had gotten the area fairly well cleared. He was feeling fairly good as the crowds were staying well back of the police tape barrier they'd quickly strung. And the gas service and emergency bomb squad was on its way, though all of that would take at least an hour.

Leland was just thinking this when a van load of disoriented Japanese tourists turned the corner through the tape barrier, heading the wrong way up the one way street trailing the barrier tape and smiling while snapping off shots with cell cameras extended out the windows. Leland ran forward to turn them around, just as the Sheriff's office exploded with a blast so powerful it rolled the van completely over on its side and then back again onto its racing wheels, propelling the van right through the front window of Kramer's Mercantile. Leland, himself, was thrown several yards backwards by the blast. When he awoke, in what seemed like seconds later, the first thing he noticed was that the star on his shirt front was tarnished, as if burnished by fire. As he absently licked his index finger to scrub it a little, he tasted the smell of his burnt finger and hair. Then he heard the screaming in Japanese. It was all quite disorienting. Then, pretty soon, there were all the reporters.

END of PART ONE: *Murders in Progress by Eldon Cene*

PART TWO: *The Cognitive Web by Eldon Cene* continues our story. It is available also on Amazon Books.

# ABOUT THE AUTHOR
## (1927 - 2012)

Eldon Cene died in Lompoc prison in 2012 after writing 31 unpublished novels. (The third to the last of which, *Murders in Progress* - the first in a trilogy - is featured here.)

Eldon often said that incarceration was "the best thing that ever happened to me. I got three squares and all the privacy any man could afford. I could never actually kick being a criminal. I'd thought it was just my true nature, until I got in here and realized that all I *really* wanted to do was to write and make up shit. After that I was through stealing. But I was still incarcerated."

He is currently buried in a potter's graveyard just outside the prison walls. "It's the only way some of us are ever getting out of here," he remarked.

He was born Sheldon Garvey in Pine Rock, Texas. But adopted Eldon Cene as his pen name, "'cause it sounded better," he said, "and like any good second story man, I was (s)eldom seen". All rights are controlled by Magic Bean Books.

- Carl Nelson, Executor